ELISA ANN PRATT

Silver Linings Trilogy: Book 1 of 3

DRAWN

Dedication:
To my inner child.
Jason & Dillon, you can do anything you put your mind to.
Steve, for your endless devotion and loving me through everything.
Mom, for always being there for me.
Grandma, your spirit lies in the stitching of my soul.
Daddy, I wish I had more time with you.
Bill, Your love remains within me, always.
Aunt Karen, Marc, David, Aim'ee, Aunt Shirley
and everyone who ever believed in my talent as a writer.
My nieces and nephews who inspire me
Theresa, my best friend

Contents

Foreword

For anyone who has ever been in a dark place.
Please know, you are never alone.
With courage to begin again,
we always find our silver linings.

Preface

This story contains sensitive material that may be disturbing to some readers for containing the following subjects: **abusive relationship, addiction, alcoholism, anxiety, sexual assault** and **sexually explicit content.** Reader discretion is advised.

Acknowledgments

Special Thanks to:

Amazing friends of Share Team & Our Block Party Crew aka The Big 6!

Your unwavering support means the absolute world to me.

I

DRAWN

Fun Facts:
My children and nephews first names were all used for characters.
Carla and Jamie's characters are based on my own personality.
I used numerology do determine my book release dates.
Family and friends will find my true life memories sprinkled throughout this story.
This is a fictional story, but the emotional aspects are my own.

Chapter 1

After my boss made me stay an hour later than my normal shift, I quickly purchased a twelve pack of Budweiser for AJ. I tried hard to ignore Nancy's glare, while she checked me out at the only cash register that was open without a line. I could almost see the little web of lies spinning behind those beady little eyes of hers. God only knew what she was thinking about me right now. She was never short of rumors to start about nearly every person she came in contact with. I honestly didn't have the time to care. I politely smiled and told her to keep the change, hoping she might extend me some grace.

As I quickly made my way out into the parking lot in search of my car, the blaring sound of a horn pierced my eardrums. I hurried my way past the driver of an old, white Ford pick-up truck who nearly hit me straight on. *I could swear his truck came out of nowhere! How could I not have seen him?* He was quite literally right in front of me.

It was a stupid rule to make the employees park on the outskirts of the parking lot. It always seemed as though management cared more about the convenience of their customers than they did about the safety of their employees.

My heart began to race as each minute passed. Surely, AJ was already furious with me for being late. He made his point crystal clear as he continued to blow my phone up with more profanity than a game of Spades in a prison yard. *Why can't he just go out and buy his own damn beer?* I mean, it's not like he was doing anything else with his life. I felt like all I was to him lately was a puppet on a string.

I knew without a doubt, for every minute I was late, the harder AJ would yank on those strings and the worse my consequences would be when the demon came out to play. After finally locating my car, I got inside and fastened my seat belt. Terrified of pissing him off any further, I stepped on the gas with all my might and raced to get home.

After pulling into my parking space, I got out of my car, holding AJ's precious beer. I decided to take a second to nurture what little beauty I had left in life. My eyes roamed into the sunlight, glistening through the branches of the old oak tree and onto the blades of the bright green grass surrounding the perimeter of our apartment building. Every now and then, these simple moments of bliss trickled seeds of hope that perhaps there might be more to life than what it had recently become for me.

~

The distinct smell of whiskey greeted me at my front door step, just like it had every other evening when I came home from work at our local Food Shop. I could hear Lynyrd Skynyrd blaring in from the stereo in our backyard. *Did he think we lived in a house on several acres of land where no one else would be bothered by the noise?* The truth was, though I may have been embarrassed by the complete lack of respect AJ had for our neighbors, there were countless nights I could recall thanking my lucky stars we that we did, in fact, have them. God forbid he ever took things too far, at least we were close enough that someone might come to my rescue.

Jack Daniels was AJ's spirit of choice, and I'm here to tell you, that spirit is no angel. I set the twelve pack down on the counter in the kitchen. One whiff and I could smell the alcohol seeping through every pore of AJ's body as he made his way across our small apartment towards me. He grabbed me by the arm like a child who needed rearing. "Get those in the fridge before I crack you a good one!" He snarled. "Best put some in the freezer, too!"

With his eyes ablaze, I could see he'd already worked himself into a fury. *Why couldn't he understand that not everything in life revolved around him?*

Every fuzzy strand of hair on my body stood up on high alert as I watched him stumble his way back out into our backyard. Slowly, my nerves began to settle when he took a seat at our patio table. I watched him pour himself another glass of whiskey before cracking open a Budweiser.

All of the downstairs apartments were lucky enough to have their own private fenced in yard. I fell in love with the view when we first arrived here in Wakefield, VA. Just over the fence, the sky aligned perfectly to watch the setting sun. I could vividly remember throwing a few bottles of Angry Orchard back with AJ as we danced in the moonlight on our first night here. It seemed like only yesterday.

Looking back, I find it rather peculiar how in the dawn of a life that was promising, we were more in love than ever. At least it seemed that way to me. Little did I know that one bad day would soon come along and completely change everything.

Like the puppet I had become, I did what AJ commanded and loaded two bottles of beer into the freezer and the remaining bottles into the crisper drawer of the fridge.

I quietly escaped into the bathroom to try and get a hot shower. After being on my feet for nine straight hours, my entire body felt sore. I let the steam roll down on my aching back as I soaked in the tranquility of my solitude. It was in these stolen moments, I felt like I could finally find some peace. *Had I escaped his aggression for one night?* I wondered. I could only hope that would have been the end of it. Tears rolled down my cheek as I released everything I had been holding on to.

Suddenly, the temperature dropped inside the bathroom as the door swung open. I had my answer far sooner than I wanted. I could hear his footsteps enter the bathroom as he unzipped his pants while letting out a loud burp. *Gross! I listened* as his urine streamed into the toilet bowl at lightning speed. With my heart pounding, I reached for the towel I had hung over the shower curtain to dry off with.

"What do you think you're doing?" AJ said as I heard the toilet flush. "You're not going anywhere!" I was so wrong to think I could honestly get a shower in peace. Frozen in place, I could only watch in horror as he tore the shower curtain open and pinned me up against the wall before I could escape. "AJ, please!" I begged. But my pleas fell on deaf ears. He was clearly was on a one way track to spread my legs apart and rip into me like some inanimate object that was his for the taking.

"Shut up, bitch! You knew you had this coming!" he said, while grabbing me by the back of my hair and slamming himself deep inside me again and again without a single shred of mercy. My hands were pinned above my head. AJ didn't seem to care one iota that my head hit the faucet when he slammed me into the shower wall. Through my tears, I could see the taint of blood streaming down into the pool of water at my feet.

All he cared about was getting what he came for, and I was grateful to find that it came to him soon. "Clean this up before you get out." He said, as he finally released me from his grasp. He took the towel I had hanging for myself, dried himself off and tossed it into the stream of the shower.

He stepped out of the shower stall, picked his clothes up off the floor and left me alone. *Thank God!* I let myself cry it out for a few minutes on the shower floor, then slowly stood back up into the stream and began scrubbing it all away, as if that somehow erased the pain. By now, the water had turned ice cold but all I cared about was removing any trace of his scent off of me.

I still felt dirty, but no amount of showering would fix that. I finally stepped out of the tub in search of a new towel to dry off with. Shivering, I wrapped myself in the warmth of the towel and slithered down the wall of our yellow painted bathroom. I brought my knees to my chest and sat myself down on the black and white checkered linoleum floor where I remained lost in contemplation for what seemed like several hours.

What did I ever do to deserve this? All I wanted was his love. Was I wrong for wanting better for us? A million questions ran through my mind, but in most of them I knew I was blaming myself for something I honestly had no control over.

I hated feeling so defenseless, especially against someone I truly loved. It was at this moment when it finally occurred to me that perhaps AJ didn't truly love me back. *He couldn't! If he did, how could he treat me this way?* Daring myself to finally come out of the bathroom, I slowly drew the door open and peeked out.

I was relieved when I found AJ passed out on our bed as I walked past our bedroom door. I quietly let myself wander into the kitchen to pull some clothes out of the dryer to wear. A pale pink sweatshirt and black spandex shorts would do just fine.

I opted to skip dinner, as my appetite was nowhere to be found. Praying I could make it through the night without any more of AJ's aggression, I curled up on the couch in our living room.

We purchased the sofa at a second hand store. It wasn't fancy, but the couch seemed functional enough to sit and watch TV. We were so much happier back then, I thought, recalling our excitement the day it was delivered. Now, the springs were all loose, and I could barely get comfortable on it.

After a few hours of tossing back and forth from side to side, haunted by the recollection of memories, good and bad, I could only wonder how I could have been so blind. *He just doesn't love me back.* The realization dawned on me that I could no longer bear another minute in this apartment or with AJ.

Chapter 2

⁓⸎⁓

T his was it, I was so done! Frantically, I began stuffing my duffle bag with as many clothes as I could fit. At any moment, he might wake up and drag me back to bed or God only knows what else. I grabbed my toothbrush and took a glance at myself in the mirror. There was blood on my lip and a nasty bruise over my brow. I looked completely disheveled in my reflection and my hair was a tousled mess. I quickly tossed my long, wavy auburn hair up in a ponytail, grabbed a ball cap, some dark shades and my keys and quietly slipped out the front door. *Where was I even going?* I had no friends in this town, he made sure of that!

I hurried to my car, quickly tossing my duffle bag and purse onto the passenger seat. I drove off into the night considering myself very lucky that AJ never woke up. *Phew!* He would never have let me leave if he had awaken. Heaven knows what I would have had to endure if I even attempted while he was up.

AJ and I came here for a fresh start just over eight months ago when his transfer got approved. He was offered a promotion to manage a construction crew with a company work truck to boot, it all seemed like a dream come true. Everything was perfect right up until his company laid half their staff off less than a month later due to permit issues. Last to come was unfortunately-first to go, AJ Stratton's dream job was no more.

At first, it was nice, coming home from work to find the house clean and dinner prepared. But after a few short weeks of being unemployed, AJ started drinking again, heavily. Thus began the onslaught of my nightmare.

By the time I came home from work, AJ would be so drunk that the tiniest thing would easily set him off. He always blamed me for encouraging him to take the transfer. In truth, I may have been selfish, secretly wanting him all to myself. I thought maybe a fresh start away from his friends might help him stop drinking every weekend.

They say hindsight is 20/20. If only I had listened to my instincts when they told me his drinking was problematic, I probably never would have moved here with him in the first place. Instead, with blind optimism, I convinced myself of the fantasy that this transfer was a possibility for our new beginning. And it was! Until everything turned sour.

~

The roads were still wet from the storm that had just passed. Because it was just past midnight, I knew that everything was closed except for the 24 hour diner. Town was only 25 minutes away, I figured I could stop there to order myself a cup of coffee.

When I arrived, it was clear that the restaurant was completely empty. The waitress was overly consumed by her make out session she was having with her boyfriend and didn't seem to notice my distress. *Good.* I wasn't ready for any explanations or judgment, anyway. I quietly slipped into the booth and pulled out my cell phone. I stared at my contacts. *Who could I even call at this hour of the night?*

I really didn't want to burden my mom with this. She'd already been through so much since Joel, my step daddy passed away unexpectedly. It was 2006 and my junior year in high school. The financial burden our family suffered made it very difficult for us to stay in our family home. It was only natural for me to offer my mother the use of my college fund to help with the bills. When that money was gone, eventually our house was foreclosed on.

After graduation, I got a job waiting tables and moved out on my own with some coworkers. This way my mom and my baby sister, Abby, could find a smaller place to live. Mama clung to anything she could keep from our old house. It all reminded her so much of the life she'd loved so dearly. I think a part of her felt that donating Joel's belongings was like saying she was ready to let go of the only true love she had ever had.

She and Abby were very cramped in that tiny apartment. *Going home was not an option.* Besides, Mama would be completely devastated if she knew that I spent the past seven months being slapped around whenever AJ decided to drink himself into oblivion. *She'd die if she knew all I had endured.* Especially after her history with my biological father, John. He was also a raging alcoholic. Mama left him when I was in preschool after coming home to find out he'd thrown away all my toys. All because I had accidentally knocked over one of his precious

11

model train sets while he was passed out drunk on the couch!

After taking another sip of my coffee, I pulled out some cash from my pocket and set it on the table. I gave a small wave, more to cover my face than to be friendly, as I stepped past the booth where the waitress and her boyfriend were sitting, cozily together. My answers were nowhere to be found in this diner or in this town. I needed to drive and think, so I hit I-95 and headed North.

I slowly allowed myself to begin processing all the damage and hurt AJ dished out towards me these past few months. The road signs were beginning to blur as my tears streamed more freely down my face. Thankfully, I had just gotten paid, so I knew I would have enough money to cover a cheap motel to stay for the night.

My job at the Food Mart didn't pay me all that much, but I was able to pick up an extra shift last week. After calling out three times this past month to hide bruises from my coworkers, I knew I had already been on my last leg. No one knew the pain I had endured. I felt so alone, guilt-ridden and ashamed.

AJ had a knack for always making me out to be the bad guy. Deep down, I knew it wasn't really all my fault, but I desperately wanted to see the AJ I had first met. And now, I was beginning to wonder, if perhaps those first couple of months we were together had all been an act. He sure laid down the charm in the beginning. I just couldn't understand how someone as charismatic as AJ was when we'd first met could turn so apathetically cold.

I was happy to finally see a sign for a few motels, so I exited the highway and stopped at the first one I could find. I sat by myself in the parking space for a few minutes as I tried to muster some strength. I needed to pull myself together before going inside.

It was late August and the air was stifling due to the record temperatures we'd been having. The breeze only exacerbated the foul stench in the air, likely from a rotting animal corpse nearby. The broken neon sign read "vac_ncy" and by the look of things, I could easily see why. There weren't many other cars in the lot. It was a run-down and gloomy-looking motel with a small pool and a handful of rusty old lounge chairs sitting just outside the reservation office. If there weren't a light on inside, I just may have found myself running for the hills.

I stepped inside to find an older lady, who was perhaps in her mid to upper fifties. Her name tag read Dionne and she was sitting behind a large front desk that was clearly made of synthetic wood. She had kind blue eyes, shoulder-length curly blonde hair and a warm smile that made me feel a little better about my choice to stay here.

"Hello. Welcome to Highway Lodge Express. Can I help you?" she asked, as though she were reading from a script.

"Yes, I would like to reserve a room, please." I replied.

"Sure thing, honey. That'd be $62.40, please," she eyed me curiously, but thankfully didn't mention my busted lip or the dark shades I was wearing in the middle of the night. I handed her my credit card. After receiving an approval for the transaction, she handed me the keys to my room.

"Room # 118.... You okay, hon?" she asked.

"Yes, thank you!" I said, making a dash for the door to escape the burden of being honest.

"Check out is at 11 AM and the WiFi is spotty," she called out to me as I was leaving. I could hear her concern in the tone of her voice, but I was in no mood for consolation. I just needed sleep.

Just as I expected, when I walked through the door, the drapery, carpet and bedspread all appeared musty and dated. It looked like the rooms hadn't been renovated since the 1980's. For the most part, though, it was clean and had just what I needed... a bed. Besides, it was only for one night, I reasoned. I just needed to figure out exactly where I was headed. For now, all I wanted was to shower and sleep away this gnawing headache.

Chapter 3

I purposely left the drapery open a little, allowing the sunlight to creep in and wake me up. I hadn't actually fallen asleep until some time after 3 AM. My dreams only haunted me, nowadays. Every blow was another piercing through my heart. It was true, I loved AJ with everything I had, but I also knew I deserved better than to have been violently raped because he'd thought I was the cause of all of his suffering. He would tell me time and time again that I deserved what I had gotten.

It was 10:14 AM when I opened my eyes and checked the time on my phone. No calls or messages. *Phew!* He was probably still sleeping and hadn't noticed I was gone yet. *Damn it! Was it almost time to check out, already?*

In hopes of buying some time to wake up and gather my thoughts a bit, I picked up the phone and dialed the operator to request a later check out. I figured I might be able to stay an extra hour since more than half the motel was empty. Thankfully, they said it was fine for me to stay until noon.

I was delighted to find that the room came equipped with a coffee maker. My excitement was short lived, however, when I discovered that my only options for fixings were powdered creamer and sweet and low. *Yuck! At least it was something to help me wake up.*

By now, since I had gotten some sleep, my headache had subsided a little. I was not looking forward to it, but I knew I was going to have to tell someone about what happened between AJ and me. A few hundred dollars was nowhere near enough to survive for very long. I needed to figure out where I was going and find a job, pronto!

I was never one to have many friends, but the ones I did have, I knew I could rely on. Heather and Amber, my old roommates, were both upset with me though because I never called them anymore. I hadn't realized just how much I had isolated myself since we moved.

I thought about Jamie for a moment. She was the only one who had any clue about my problems with AJ. She called me just a few months ago to tell me she'd finally moved out of her dorm when she moved into her new apartment in Boston, where she was studying law. She sounded so happy and I was so excited for her.

It was unfortunate that our call ended abruptly when AJ and I started arguing. I swear, he always found a way to steal my attention back to him and away from anyone else that may have had it. Jamie tried calling me three more times that week and each time I only replied to her by text. I just told her I was working and promised to call her back. Each time I promised, I lied. I basically ghosted my best friend because I was embarrassed and didn't want to face the truth about AJ. I should have answered her calls. I felt horrible for not calling her back, but I knew that if there was anyone in this world who could draw the truth out of me, Jaime was that person.

Jamie Foster and I met in the sixth grade. I was smart, but I hated doing homework. One morning before school, I walked up to her and asked to copy her Math homework and she was nice enough to let me. It was from there that our friendship blossomed.

We shared everything with each other all throughout our childhood. I always felt very blessed to have her in my life. She was always kind and never made me feel inadequate, even after I made the decision to get a job instead of going to college. When I told her, she was disappointed because she always thought I had so much potential as a writer, but she also understood my situation.

Chapter 4

J amie was one of those girls who literally had it all. She was beautiful, caring and very smart. Every year she made the honor roll, so it came as no surprise to anyone when she had her choice of any college she wanted to go to. I was incredibly sad to see her leave for Boston, but also very happy for her and her future. There was no doubt in my mind, she was going to make a great lawyer one day. I really missed having her around to confide in, though. I knew she'd know exactly what I should do.

I found her number in my phone, took a deep breath in and held it before pressing down on the send button to call her. I nearly lost my courage and hung up when she answered on the fourth ring.

"Carla?! Is that you?" She asked. I choked up as soon as I heard her voice on the other end of the line. After some silence, I cleared my throat.

"Yes, yes, it's me." I replied.

"How the hell are ya?! Where have you been? Are you alright?" Jamie asked, throwing questions out like daggers.

"I'm okay." I said.

"No you're not, I can hear it in your voice. What's going on? Whose ass do I need to kick?!" she exclaimed.

"It's OK, Jamie, I'm fine. At least, I will be. Listen, do you have a few minutes to talk?" I asked, knowing very well that she wouldn't dare let me off the line until she knew exactly what the matter was.

"Of course, I've been trying to get a hold of you for months! I do have a class in about an hour, but please tell me what's got you so upset. Is everything alright with you and AJ? I swear I'll come down there and kick his ass, too, if I have to!"

Hearing her voice brought me so much peace, and normally I'd probably laugh at her response, but the truth was, she was spot on. My problems with AJ were exactly what brought me to the moment I was in now. I briefly explained to her what happened and told her where I was. She started planning aloud to ditch her classes to come down and get me in an instant. After finally convincing her that I was okay to drive myself, she made me promise to come up to Boston and stay with her until I could figure out what to do. Although I thought the idea seemed a little crazy, I agreed because I honestly didn't have any other solutions. After giving me her address, she made me promise to check in with her by text every few hours to let her know I was okay.

Chapter 5

T he drive to Boston wasn't all that bad. It took me just over
seven hours to get to the address Jamie gave me. I found the
parking garage easily and the lobby with the elevator, just as
she had mentioned. Since I left in such a hurry, there wasn't all that
much for me to carry, just my duffle bag with my belongings.

The building was modern looking and very well kept. Even the
elevator smelled of fresh pressed linens. I could already tell that Jamie's
apartment would be far more fancier than my apartment was with AJ.
Her parents were pretty well off. I was sure they were helping her pay
the rent.

I typed in the security pin code Jamie gave me and hit the button for
the seventh floor. Apartment 709 wasn't far from the elevator. As I
approached Jamie's door, I couldn't ignore the knot forming in the pit
of my stomach. *What was I afraid of? Jamie was my oldest and dearest
friend.* In direct combat with my nerves, I rang the bell.

It didn't take long for Jamie to answer the door and when she did, she didn't speak a word. Instead, she extended both her arms out to embrace me. She hugged me long enough for me to begin to relax… *This was exactly what I needed, my best friend.*

"Come in, Come in!" she cried. Take those sunglasses off and let me see you! It's only been what, like forever?"

She came down to visit over Christmas break the year before last, so it had been nearly two years since we'd last seen each other. I had only met AJ a few months prior to her visit and things were going pretty well between us at the time. I vividly remember Jamie giving me her famous "BFF seal of approval" just before she left to go back to Boston.

The minute I took my sunglasses off, I could see that little line in her brow begin to furrow. She was pissed, as I knew she would be. If any guy had done this to her, I'd be pissed too. Jamie knew me like no one else. She knew I would need time to process my feelings before I could really talk about them so she didn't press me any further.

"Well, now that you're here, let me show you around my new place." she said, relieving me of the weight of my bag from my shoulder.

If circumstances had been different, I know she would have been very excited to see me. It's not that she wasn't, I could just tell she was trying her best to conceal how she really felt as she gave me the tour of her new apartment. It was much larger than I had anticipated, with two spacious bedrooms and two full bathrooms.

The decor screamed Jamie Foster. She'd always been a fan of nature. There were animals and mountain-scapes in frames all along the walls, carpet in the bedrooms and hard-wood floors throughout the rest of the apartment. I had an inkling that this was Jamie's way of having the best of both worlds, city and country.

The living room was furnished with a cozy wrap-around couch, a mid-sized flat screen TV that hung above a chestnut entertainment center and a large, fluffy white rug laid out in the center of the hardwood floor. On each side of the couch, there were matching side tables that held potted plants.

The kitchen was galley styled, but large enough to cook a gourmet meal and fully stocked with anything she could ever need. She and I both loved to cook, so that wasn't very surprising. I was impressed. She really had everything put together. It made me feel a little sad inside that I didn't. I wasn't envious of her, I was simply disappointed in myself for not being further in life than I'd expected, by now.

"Well, what do you think? Do you like it?" She asked.

"It's beautiful, Jamie. I had no idea your apartment would be this big. You did a fabulous job in decorating." I said, truly meaning every word.

"Why don't we bring your bag to your room so I can help you unpack." She offered. I never imagined having my own room, I figured at best, I'd be shacking up on her couch for a few weeks.

"My parents wanted me to have a spare bedroom for whenever they decided to fly up for a visit. So there's actually a pretty comfy queen size bed in there for you to sleep in. You can use the bureau and the closet for your clothes. The bathroom in the hallway can be yours too." She added.

"Are you sure it's not a problem?" I asked. "I really don't want to put you or your parents out."

It was plain to see, Jamie was delighted to provide whatever I needed in my time of crisis. She was just that way, always caring and nurturing. We both had those traits in common. I think that's why we always got along so well, together.

After all these years, we had only gotten into one fight throughout our entire friendship. It happened when we were in the eighth grade when our History teacher let us pair up for a cookie continent project. Unfortunately, we both wanted to be in complete control over the project, the little perfectionists that we were. Jamie wound up leaving because we couldn't agree on anything.

The funniest part about it was that our teacher, Mrs. Crawford, who always seemed to have it out for me, wound up throwing our project in the trash in front of the whole class. She gave us both a failing grade because we'd forgotten one stupid river. I never knew what Mrs. Crawford's deal was with me, but I was so mad that day. Not only did we both get a failing grade, we also never got a chance to eat the damn cookie! Afterwards, all we could do was laugh about how silly we'd gotten over it. Other than that, our friendship had survived many outsiders who had come and gone.

"This is not even close to what I envisioned when you had asked me to come stay with you. I thought you would have a small one bedroom or studio apartment. This place is stunning! Really, it is Jamie. Thank you so much for inviting me here." I said with tears in my eyes.

"Now don't you start, Carla, you're gonna make me cry," she said. "How about we go grab a bite to eat, I'm starving! And you've been driving all day, so I'm sure you're hungry too. There's a great little pizza place just around the corner we can walk to, how does that sound?" She asked.

"Pizza sounds great!" She was right, I was starving. I agreed and soon we were out the door.

Chapter 6

I thought it was pretty cool that anything we could ever want or need was right within walking distance. We barely walked for ten minutes before arriving at the pizza place Jamie mentioned. At least it wasn't as hot in Boston as it had been in Virginia, the weather was actually beautiful. Upper seventies with a light breeze. Perfect for a stroll down the block. *I could get used to this.* I was already starting to feel so much better. I had never been to Boston before. Clearly, Jamie was in her element here. She was always fascinated by the big city.

The pizza place was charmingly small, with only a few booths to sit and eat in and a walk up counter that displayed a window of all the different pizza pies that were already made for people who preferred to order by the slice. Behind the counter, we could see a guy tossing pizza dough up in the air as we each placed our orders. Jamie and I decided to take our slices to go so we could eat back at her apartment and catch up. When we got back, Jamie said she had a little surprise for me.

"Guess what we're going to watch?" She asked.

I was well aware of her extensive collection of DVD's she had started back while we were in high school. It was only a few minutes before I had my answer as she loaded it into the DVD player and pushed play.

Pretty Woman was one of our most treasured favorites! We must have watched it at least a dozen times together. Movies had always been our 'go to' whenever either of us were upset. We'd always get together, make a boatload of snacks and watch the classics.

Jamie had a way of making me feel right at home. My favorite food, favorite movie and my very best friend. What more could I want or need? Apparently, I didn't make it through the whole film before passing out on the couch. She woke me up when the movie was over so I could go to bed.

As I lay there, I couldn't help but reflect. All in all, today had really shaped into a pretty pleasant day, a stark contrast to the one before. *Was the universe telling me I had made the right decision to come to Boston?* Only time would tell, but for now, I felt safe and comfortable and that was all I could really ask for.

Chapter 7

~~~~~~~~~~~

The next morning, I felt so refreshed. I don't know if it was the luxury I was wrapped in or the fact that I had barely gotten any sleep the night before, but I could swear, I hadn't slept this well in months! The high quality mattress I lay in was dressed in 1000 thread count sheets, feather pillows and a cozy down comforter that smelled deliciously of lavender and sage. I reached over to unplug my phone from the charger on the nightstand and turn it on. Jamie suggested I turn it off when I arrived. *Boy, was she ever so right?!*

There were 14 missed calls and 23 text messages from AJ. *Ugh…* Already, I felt like I couldn't breathe. Summoning her sixth sense, Jamie came into my room and grabbed my phone from my hands the moment I started to panic.

"Don't even think about it! It's Saturday and we have plans!" she said.

"We do?" I asked.

"Yes! I booked us each an appointment at the salon for manicures and pedicures and we are going to the cell store right afterwards to change your number!"

"We are?" I asked, yawning.

"Yes! And you're lucky I'm not making you go to the police station to press charges and get a restraining order on that asshole." she said.

A part of me still felt sorry for AJ and desperately wanted to call him to let him know I was alright, but if I knew Jamie, she'd never allow that! I honestly couldn't blame her. If the situation had been reversed, I'd feel the same way. Hesitantly, I let her take the lead and handed her my phone.

"Don't you think I should at least text him back and let him know I'm OK?" I asked.

"Absolutely not, Missy! I love you to death, honey, but your heart is what landed you in this position in the first place. AJ *will* get over it, and believe me, your future self will thank me. Now let's go get you dressed and ready to go! Our appointment is in 45 minutes!"

"I don't think I packed any other shoes with me, I was in such a hurry to leave. All I have are my ratty old sneakers." I said, feeling somewhat embarrassed by my misfortune.

"Already taken care of. I have a cute little sundress and some strappy sandals for you to wear, today. It's time you get out and go have some fun for a change!" She said as she quickly produced them both in each of her hands. She really did think of everything.

"I made you a cup of coffee, just how you like it. It's on the dining room table, you can meet me there when you finish getting dressed."

Jamie may have gone a little overboard in taking care of me, but I found her doting on me to be endearing. A welcoming distraction from my dark and twisted thoughts.

"Thanks," I said, as I pulled the covers down off of me.

The sunlight was beaming in through the bedroom window. I tried to get ready as fast as I could, knowing all too well how Jamie hated to be late to anything. We were a lot alike in some ways and polar opposites in others. I was rarely on time for anything, but for all she'd done for me since I'd gotten here, the least I could do was ensure we didn't arrive late for our appointment.

Chapter 8

I thoroughly enjoyed the foot massage included in the pedicure service. The nail tech told me I had a lot of tension in my feet. I was so relaxed that somehow, I let Jamie convince me to reach out to my mom. I agreed to let Mama know where I was, at the very least.

After our spa appointment, we went to the cellular store to change my number, as planned. As soon as my new phone was ready, I sent a quick text message to Mama, giving her my new number. I also told her I would try to give her a call later today.

I was beginning to feel my stomach growl when Jamie asked, "Are you hungry?" *There goes that sixth sense again*! I laughed to myself.

"Starving!" I said.

"Great! We can have brunch at the Plaza Cafe! It's a local hot spot, so hopefully the line won't be too long. Their Croissant French Toast is to die for, you're gonna love it!" she said, sounding excited. By then, it was already 1 o'clock, so the line she'd mentioned was already gone. I was happy because I really was hungry. Typically, I would have already eaten breakfast an hour after having my coffee.

When we arrived at the Plaza Cafe, Jamie told the hostess that we didn't need menus as we each took our seats at the table we were directed to.

"Trust me," Jamie said, "French Toast is a must for a first timer!" She really didn't have to convince me, I was already sold.

"If you say so, French Toast it is! I'll have a coffee and a small glass of orange juice as well, please." I said to the waitress as she scribbled it down onto her notepad.

"I will also have the french toast, but just coffee for me, please." Jamie added.

When the waitress left our table, I noticed a pretty blonde girl staring at us from across the cafe. She caught me looking in her direction and a moment later, she stood up and proceeded towards our table.

"Jamie Foster?!" she exclaimed.

Jamie whipped her head around to see who it was. "Oh my gosh! Breana Marshall! How are ya?!" She said, as she quickly stood up to hug Breana. I had no idea who Breana was. Jamie never mentioned her to me before. Then again, my head had been buried in the sand from nearly everyone I had ever been close to, as of late.

"Breana, this is my very best friend from middle school, Carla. Carla, this is Breana. She and I had a few classes together during freshman

31

year. She's also a good friend. Although the only time I ever see her, here lately, is when I book an appointment to get my hair done. Breana is also my beautician."

"It's so nice to meet you." Breana said, smiling. She appeared about as tall as I was. She had sun-kissed, chin length blonde hair, brown eyes and a friendly smile. Her demeanor seemed genuine and nice.

"It's nice to meet you too!" I replied as I stood up to shake her hand.

"Come sit with us." Jamie said as she pulled out a chair for Breana to sit down.

"OK, but only for a few minutes," she said. "I'm here having brunch with my boyfriend, Ryan. I told him I wouldn't be too long. I just had to come by to say hello. It's been so long since I'd seen you, Jamie. How have you been? I see your hair has grown out quite a bit. You really ought to come by for a trim sometime, soon."

"I know, it is getting long isn't it?" Jamie agreed. "I'm doing great! I just got a new apartment up on Main Street! Things have really been looking up for me lately and they just got a whole lot better, now that Carla's here!" Seeing the genuine excitement on Jamie's face completely secured my warm, welcome.

Breana eyed me over for a moment and must have taken notice of the bruise above the rim of my sunglasses. "What happened to you? Did you just have eye surgery?" Clearly, she had an eye for detail and was bold enough to ask. Nonetheless, it was a fair question. Jamie gave me a blank stare, letting me take the lead on whether I wanted to tell her what really happened. I didn't want to start things off by lying to someone who appeared to be a good friend to Jamie, so I opened up and told her the truth. It was plain to see that Jamie trusted Breana by how warm and friendly she was towards her. One thing about Jamie, if she didn't like you, you knew it. She wasn't the type to sugarcoat or be phony.

"Actually, I came here because my boyfriend and I got in a fight, back home." I said without going into details. I didn't need to. She'd already seen the bruise.

"Oh, honey! I'm so sorry to hear that! Are you OK?" Breana asked, looking truly concerned.

"I'm OK, thanks." I said. "I'm just a little shaken up, but Jamie has been taking real good care of me ever since I got here."

"Well, that doesn't surprise me, one bit! Jamie's a good friend. She always has been to me, anyway. She's helped me through more than a few break ups and by the looks of your eye there, it sounds like you made the right decision to leave the guy."

Although I never did like feeling pitied and was still processing how I felt about my situation with AJ, I could see Breana was being friendly and supportive and that she meant well. Jamie had always been a great judge of character. Breana seemed OK in my book, too.

"Listen, Jamie. It's been so long since we have had any real time to catch up! What are you guys doing later? Do you wanna come out with us to this new club? It's called Hush! It's going to be so much fun! Ryan's best friend, Alex, is going to DJ there tonight for their grand opening. He was able to score us some free entries and told me to bring whoever

I wanted. All I have to do is give them your names for the list at the door."

Jamie's eyes lit up, and although I didn't think I was quite ready to go dancing at a nightclub, I could see that she really wanted to go.

"Oh, I don't know, Breana, Carla just got into town yesterday. I don't know if she'd be up to a night out clubbing just yet." Jamie answered. She was protecting me as she always had. I didn't want to damper their excitement and I knew that if I didn't go, Jamie wouldn't either.

"We'd love to go!" I blurted out before Jamie could say another word. "I just don't know about going out with my face looking the way it does, people will stare at me." I said.

"Don't worry about that hon, I've got that covered! You'd be surprised what a little foundation and concealer can do! Besides, it's kind of what I do!" Breana laughed. "So you two can meet us at my place at 8 o'clock and we can all get ready together. We're gonna have so much fun!" She said and with that, she made her way back over to her boyfriend who was patiently waiting for her at their own table back in the corner.

"Are you sure about this, Carla?" Jamie asked me, once Breana was gone.

"Absolutely, I'm looking forward to it!" I said. Apparently, I must have been quite convincing because Jamie totally bought it. Truthfully, I was a little nervous. It was a lot to take in, between the fight with AJ, coming to Boston and now we were going out clubbing. It all seemed a little fast for me. I really didn't want to be a burden though, or cramp on Jamie's lifestyle on my second day here, so Saturday night clubbing was the plan.

Chapter 9

❦

I couldn't believe how right Breana was about makeup! I rarely wore anything more than lip gloss, eye-shadow and little mascara on special occasions. I was surprised to see how well the foundation and concealer she applied on me had completely made my bruises disappear. In fact, if I didn't still feel a little sore, It would appear as if nothing had even happened.

Breana's collection of club dresses to choose from was surely one to admire. One look at my reflection in the mirror proved that I was beginning to feel more confident. The sparkly silver dress and black studded stiletto heels she let me borrow easily fit me like a glove. I decided on the disco ball looking dress because it reminded me of New Years Eve. *Why the hell not?* I thought, as I tried to convince myself I might be ready to add a little sparkle back into my life.

Ryan, Breana's boyfriend, rented us a limousine to take us to and from the club so we could all have a good time and not worry about driving ourselves home. I'd only been in a limo twice before, both times were for funerals. The idea of riding in one for pleasure brought some genuine excitement to the evening for me.

"You girls look hot!" Ryan said as we all made our way outside to wait for the limo. Ryan was tall, had mousy brown hair and brown eyes. Together, he and Breana looked like a model couple as they were both very attractive, especially standing next to one another.

"Thank you, Baby! Not too shabby, yourself, stud!" Breana said, giving him a quick love tap on the ass.

"So, tell me, how long have y'all been together? Where did you guys meet?" Jamie asked, inquisitively as we all piled inside the limousine. I fully appreciated the purple and green neon light embellishment added to each side of the car as it clearly distinguished a different set of ambiance from my previous limo riding experience.

Breana and Ryan both looked at each other and laughed. "Well, believe it or not, Ryan's Grandmother hooked us up! She's a very good client of mine. I think she may have grown tired of hearing my horror stories from all the guys I met on the dating apps. We've been together for about four months now. I honestly couldn't be happier!" she said, giving Ryan a wink.

"Me either, Gram's got great taste! Who knew?!" Ryan chimed back.

Chapter 10

When we arrived at the club, the line was wrapped around the block. I shuddered at the thought of standing there all that time in the stiletto heels Breana let me borrow. My toes already felt like they were on fire. I rarely wore heels anymore. AJ and I hadn't gone anywhere in ages, it seemed. I figured we would have to wait at least an hour before we could get in. Thankfully, and to everyone's surprise, Ryan's friend, Alex, came to our rescue. He took us all around to the back door entrance and told us we could skip the line. *Phew!*

Ryan introduced us all just before we scurried past the crowd. Alex stood a few inches taller than Ryan. He had brown eyes, dark brown hair and a goatee to match. He had that scruffy kind of grunge look to his style, but in a clean way. Definitely a creative type, I thought in my first impression.

"My girl, Mandy, will be here a little later. I told her you guys were coming so she doesn't have to be by herself. She just got off work. She had to go home first to get ready" He said to Ryan and Breana.

"She's such a sweet girl, we'd be happy to keep her entertained." Breana said to Alex as we all entered the club.

The lights were still on inside the club. The workers were still setting things up for the grand opening. It was kinda cool, because we were able to get a good look at behind the scenes and all the details that were involved. Thank God we weren't still in line, I thought to myself as I took notice that they still hadn't let anyone inside the club yet.

The ceilings were set high and adorned with crystal chandeliers. There were two separate bar sections that were off to each side of the club. A large stage and two smaller side stages had been set in the center of a large circular dance floor. Aligning the outskirts of the dance floor, there were several red and blue half moon shaped lounge sofas with cocktail tables. Whoever designed the club must have had the upper class in mind for the clientele, as every detail appeared to be of the utmost quality. The place was absolutely stunning! We were soon directed by Alex to wait in the lounge area while he went to set up his DJ equipment.

"The bar will be open any minute. Just tell them you're here with me and you will all get your first drink 'on the house'!" He said before heading back towards the rear entrance of the club. I was relieved to finally get off my feet for a few minutes as I took my seat on one of the sofas that was surprisingly comfortable for being art deco. A few minutes after Alex got the music going, the lights were dimmed and security began to let people inside the club.

"So what's everyone drinking?" Ryan asked. "I'll go grab them before the bar gets too busy."

"I'll have my usual. Cosmo, please!" Breana replied.

"Malibu and coke for me," Jamie answered.

"Lightweight!" Ryan remarked, jokingly.

"I guess I'll have a vodka sea breeze, just ask them to make sure they use grapefruit juice, not pineapple juice." I added.

I was never much of a drinker, I typically went for a single glass of red wine or Sangria on occasion. If ever I did choose to indulge in spirits, it was always vodka for me. I had sworn off drinking away from home a long time ago, when AJ crashed my car into a median one night on our way home from a night out drinking. He'd fallen asleep at the wheel while I was passed out in the passenger seat. The thump jolted me awake and scared the living daylights out of me. Thankfully no one got hurt. Just my tire, the rim and obviously my bank account when I had to get it fixed. I was barely 21 at the time, but still, I should have known better than to let AJ drive us home.After that incident, I told myself I would be the designated driver from there on out.

Just thinking about how many mornings I'd spent cleaning up AJ's vomit was enough to make me nauseous. The smell of dark liquor gave me post traumatic stress... *But we aren't thinking about AJ tonight, remember?* I thoughtfully reminded myself. I had every intention of loosening up to try and have a good time with everyone, the last thing I wanted was to be a party pooper.

A few minutes later, Ryan returned carrying our drinks on a tray he must have borrowed from the bar. The first sip of my drink burned the back of my throat. "This tastes really strong!" I said, coughing.

"That's probably because I gave the bartender a hundred dollar tip before she made our drinks!" Ryan laughed. "I mean, they were free to begin with. The least I could do was give her a decent tip!"

His reasoning did seem justifiable. We learned that Ryan spent a good amount of time serving and bar-tending prior to becoming a general manager at his restaurant, on our ride up to the club in the limo.

"My drink tastes delicious! You did good, Babe." Breana said as she leaned in to give him a kiss.

"Thanks, Ryan," said Jamie.

After a few more sips of my drink, the ice melted a little and thankfully, my taste buds adjusted.

"Yes, thank you!" I chimed in, I didn't want to come off as being ungrateful. "It actually tastes a lot better now." I said, trying to shake my awkwardness.

The music had a great vibe. As it turned out, Alex was a phenomenal DJ. I could finally feel myself beginning to relax as the liquor began to make its way through my system.

"Let's go dance!" Jamie said, nearly jumping to her feet to take my hand. Although I felt a little reluctant to go anywhere in these heels, I didn't want to steal away from her excitement, so I sucked it up for Jamie's sake.

"You two go have fun, we'll stay here and wait for Mandy to show up. We'll meet you guys out there!" Breana called out as Jamie pulled me out onto the dance floor.

~

I was surprised to see how many people were already out on the dance floor, the club had literally just opened.

"This is so much fun!" Jamie shouted over the music. I mostly felt silly, but tried my best to keep up with Jamie. Jamie pointed out to me that there were several guys watching us from the bar area. We both giggled and were having a great time when all of a sudden, a group of them began to crowd around us.

I don't know why it seemed so unexpected to me that I might have to dance with a guy. After all, that's what people do in a nightclub. I guess I just wasn't prepared for how I would react. It wasn't until one of them grabbed me by my waist and swung me around to see his face that my stomach began to flip flop. Was it the aroma of his cologne or the smell of Jack Daniels on his breath? Maybe it was the way he grabbed me in such a possessive way… whatever it was, my nerves were in full panic mode.

I glanced over at Jamie who appeared to be having the time of her life. *Why did I feel like I couldn't breathe?* I broke free from his grasp and awkwardly blurted "I have to go, I'm sorry!" And with that, I kicked off the heels I was wearing and ran off to go find a bathroom.

I just knew I had to get away from the crowd. Tears were stinging my cheeks as I flew past the bar where I could feel several people staring at me. Finally, I saw the sign for the restrooms.

The bathroom attendant saw me run inside the stall. "Is everything OK, Miss?" she asked through the door. "I'm fine!" I called out, but I couldn't stop sobbing or make the sense of panic subside. A few minutes later, I heard a familiar voice.

"Carla! It's me, open up!" *Damn it!* Jamie had to have seen me run off and come after me. *Shit!*

"I'm OK, Jamie," I replied back, but the croak in my voice made it clear that I wasn't.

"No, you're not! What's going on? Open up!" She insisted.

After a minute, I opened the stall. I must have looked like a hot mess, because I could see it written all over Jamie's face. "What happened? Did that guy hurt you or touch you inappropriately?" She asked, determined to go set things straight.

"Yes... I mean No! It wasn't like that, Jamie. I just sort of panicked. I'm so sorry, I don't want to ruin your night out. Go back out there, I'll be fine in here for a little while." I said.

"No way, Jose! I'm not leaving you here like this... Absolutely not! And you didn't ruin my night. I knew it was too soon for you to be out like this. How could I be so foolish to think that you were ready?" She said as she clearly felt responsible for my suffering. I didn't want her to feel bad for wanting to be here. That was the last thing I wanted.

"It's not your fault, Jamie. Please don't beat yourself up over it. I'll be OK in a few minutes, I may just need to sit out on the dancing part." I said. I really wanted her to get back out there and have a good time.

"No, no... I'm calling us an UBER." Jamie said as she reached inside her purse to find her phone. One thing about Jamie, when she made decisions, she rarely backed out of them. I figured I'd better not argue with her and make things worse.

"Besides, this club ain't going anywhere anytime soon. I'm sure we can come back another time. Just wait here a minute while I let Breana and Ryan know that we're leaving. And don't you worry, I'll just tell them I'm not feeling well and that you don't want me to go home alone." She said, as I watched her hand the bathroom attendant a twenty dollar bill and asked her to keep an eye on me for a few minutes.

I felt horrible inside. Jamie knew I'd be embarrassed if her friends knew we were leaving on account of me, but she was right as usual. I needed more time to heal. I just hated that I was dampening Jamie's life now too.

We were both pretty quiet on the ride home. Jamie held my hand the entire time. I really was blessed to have such a sweet and caring friend. "Come on, I'll fix us some mac and cheese." She said, when we arrived at her apartment building. I certainly wasn't going to turn that down.

"That sounds perfect." I said.

"I think we've had enough excitement for one night, anyway, huh?" She asked.

"Yeah." I agreed. "Thanks for taking such good care of me, Jamie. You've been a life saver throughout all of this, I don't know how I will ever thank you enough!"

"First off, there's no thanks needed," she said. "That's what best friends are for and I know you would do the same for me in a heartbeat!" She was damn right, I would.

Chapter 11

After a night of tossing and turning, I finally decided to go ahead and get out of bed before the crack of dawn. Since it was Sunday, I knew I would have a chance to take a nap later in the afternoon. I quietly made my way into the kitchen in search of coffee. I wanted to cook breakfast for Jamie to show my gratitude for everything she had done for me. She had always been an early bird, so this would probably be my only opportunity to surprise her.

I swear, she must have smelled the bacon, because as soon as it was ready, she was in the cupboard grabbing a coffee mug.

"Wow! You're up early... What's all this?" Jamie asked. She seemed more surprised by the fact that I was up before she was on a Sunday.

"Good morning," I said. "I hope you don't mind, but I wanted to cook us some breakfast. Just some scrambled eggs, bacon and toast. I also cut up some strawberries."

"Do I mind? Never!" she laughed. "It smells divine, Thank you! I appreciate it. Would you mind if we have some coffee first?"

"Not at all!" I replied. I was honestly grateful that we were both on the same page.

"Great, how about we go sit outside on the balcony?" she asked.

"Balcony? Sure, that sounds great," I answered.

The sun was just beginning to rise over Boston. The air was crisp and cool to the touch and if you listened closely, you could hear the faint chatter of the birds in the trees from the park nearby. I could almost bet Jamie intended to skip over the view of the city from her terrace in her tour of her apartment for this very moment.

"Oh my God, Jamie! This view is stunning!"

Jamie smiled. "I knew you'd love it! It is perfect, isn't it? This is my morning spot."

"Well, I can certainly see why!" I said, staring out over the balcony at the strikingly beautiful warm orange hues spread across the violet skyline.

We each took a seat in the tan colored chaise lounges she had furnished on her porch. The pair of chairs were joined by a small, wrought iron coffee table painted in white. On the side of each chair, there were ficus tree plants that were both at least 4 feet tall. I could imagine this would be a perfect place for me to sit and read or write.

I hadn't written anything in a long time. In fact, I was beginning to think I may have lost my talent, altogether. It occurred to me then, there were many aspects of myself that seemed to have fallen away from me after meeting AJ.

"Hey, did you happen to see the guy I was dancing with last night?" Jamie asked, interrupting my thoughts.

"You mean that tall, handsome, guy in the yellow shirt?" I asked.

"Yep! That's the one!" she said. "He actually gave me his number as I was making my way back to come find you. His name is Dillon." The gleam in Jamie's eyes told me she must have been really into him.

"Really? That's great!" I said. I suppose I hadn't entirely ruined her night, after all. At least now, she would have an opportunity to explore things further with him.

"He said he would text me today, so I guess we'll see what happens." She said.

"Any guy would be lucky to be with you, Jamie. I'm sure you'll be hearing from him very soon." I said.

I was beginning to feel my spirit come alive again. Jamie's revelation this morning was exactly what I needed to hear in terms of letting myself off the hook from my conscience, still heavily laden with guilt from the night before.

"Are you hungry yet?" I asked, feeling hungry myself.

"Starved! Let's go inside and eat!" she answered.

We decided to take our breakfast over to the sofa in the living room. Jamie popped in an old cult classic to her DVD player, The Breakfast Club. One of my personal favorites!

"How appropriate?" I said, as I sat down on the couch with my plate of food.

"Hey, thanks for cooking us breakfast this morning. " Jamie said, stuffing her mouth with a whole strip of bacon.

When the movie was over, my eyes were getting tired.

"I didn't sleep very well last night, would you mind terribly if I go lay back down?" I asked, yawning.

"Not at all, I have some studying to do, anyway." she said.

Chapter 12

❧

I t was nearly 4:30 PM when my phone rang and woke me up. *Oh no! I never called Mama!*

"Hi Mama!" I said, trying hard not to sound like I was sleeping.

"Hi honey, Did I wake you?" she asked. *Damn it!* I laughed to myself.

"Yeah, you got me, I was taking a nap." I replied. "But it's fine, I didn't want to sleep in this late, anyway. How are you?"

"I'm fine, honey. I was waiting for you to call me yesterday. I was a little worried, but figured I would give you until today to call me back. How are you doing? And what on God's green earth are you doing up in Boston?" she asked.

"Oh mama, I didn't want you to worry about me. Really, I'm fine. I'm here visiting Jamie. She moved out of the dorm and into this gorgeous apartment! You should see it, it has Jamie written all over it!"

I was still on the fence on whether I wanted to let her know about the fighting that had been going on between AJ and me.

"That's lovely. And what about AJ? Is he there with you, too?" she asked. *Shit!* I was hoping the mention of Jamie and her new apartment would distract her.

"Well," I couldn't completely lie to her, I had to tell her something. Maybe I could just leave out a few details that might cause her to worry. "Actually, no. He's still at our apartment in Wakefield. The truth is… Mama, we weren't exactly getting along so well."

"Oh? I'm sorry to hear that baby, I'm sure it had to be pretty rough for you to have left town like that. I know things must be difficult with the lay off and everything. What about your job? Did they just let you take time off? How can you afford to take a vacation right now with AJ being out of work?" She asked. Question after question hitting me like daggers that were produced in factory, and all the right ones. *Of course!* I could already hear the concern laced inside her voice. *Why were mothers so good at being detectives?* There's no escaping the absolute truth now, I thought.

By the grace of God, Jamie heard my conversation from the other room and quickly came to my rescue. She grabbed the phone and turned it on speaker phone so we could both hear.

"Hi Corrine! How are you? How's Abby doing?" She asked.

"Hi Jamie! I'm good and Abby's doing great, thanks for asking! Can you believe she's a sophomore in high school already? My babies are growing up so fast!" Mama replied, with a slight tinge of sadness to her tone. "Carla tells me things are going really well for you in Boston. How's school going?"

"We're just starting Fall quarter now. School is going great, so far! I still have a little ways to go, but we're moving right along! Please tell Abby I said hello... I've missed Carla so much, she and I are having a blast! It's so nice to have my best friend back! Here, I'll let you say goodbye to your daughter. It was so nice to talk to you!" She said, handing me back the phone. Jamie had a real talent for diversions.

"Hey Mama, it's me, Carla. Where's Abby?" I asked.

"She went to the mall with her friends. I think they're going to see a movie." She answered.

"Oh, okay. Please tell her I love her. I'll talk to you guys again soon. Love you Mama!" I said with the transfer of some of Jamie's energy.

"I love you too, Baby! You two have fun and take care! Please don't forget to keep in touch!" she said.

"You know I will... Love you, Mama! Bye!" I said and hung up before she remembered all the questions she'd asked me before.

"You really are a lifesaver, Jamie! Thanks for taking over for me! It worked like a charm!" I said, feeling relieved.

"Of course!" she winked. "I know you're not ready to tell her about everything just yet, but you definitely ought to, when you are."

"I will." I said. I did plan on telling Mama at some point, I just needed more time to figure out what I was going to do with my life first.

"Hey, do you think you might be able to help me update my resume? I asked. "I wanna start looking for a job tomorrow. I don't know what I'm doing or where I'm going yet, but I do know I'll need money regardless. I was thinking of checking out the restaurant scene. Those types of jobs are relatively easy to find and cash tips come quicker than a paycheck. I was also thinking about looking for some office type work, since I'm here in the big city."

"Absolutely!" She answered, seemingly surprised by my new found energy. "I know! We should create two separate resumes for you. One that will accentuate the service industry and one for your office experience. I think they'll help you find what you're looking for." she said.

"Okay, that sounds great!" I said, feeling grateful for having such a supportive friend.

"You know, you *can* stay here as long as you like! If my parents come down to visit, you'll just have to sleep on the couch while they're here. They never stay more than a few days anyway. Besides, the quicker we find you a job, the faster you'll grow to love it here. I promise you will!" Jamie paused as if she realized she may have been getting ahead of herself. "You know, I totally understand if you decide to go back to stay with your mom and Abby in Virginia. But now that I finally have you here, I'm going to make it my mission to convince you to stay!"

"Awe, thank you!" I said, smiling. It was so nice to feel my presence being welcomed for a change.

Somewhere in the back of my mind, I still had lingering thoughts about returning to my apartment with AJ. *Was it familiarity, or did I actually miss him?* I wondered. I knew Jamie would probably kill me just for thinking about it. For now, I would tuck that idea back where it came from in the back of my mind.

Chapter 13

Monday morning seemed fit to paint the town with my resume. Jamie gave me full reign of her closet for any clothes I might need before she left for school. We both knew I didn't have all that much with me. Another good reason to find work, I thought. If I did choose to stay in Boston, I would definitely need some new clothes.

I opened the door inside Jamie's bedroom to find a walk-in closet full of various types of clothing. Everything looked so neat and organized. She had everything color coordinated and far easier to find in comparison to my own closet, back home, where my clothes were lucky to meet a hanger. I chose a soft lavender blouse and a nice pair of stretchy dark washed jeans.

The bruise above my eyebrow was slowly beginning to lighten up, so it wasn't all that difficult to cover up with the makeup Breana was kind enough to let me keep. I added some mascara and lip gloss to finish things off.

We printed off several copies of my resume, so I tucked them all neatly inside the folder Jamie gave me and walked out the door, determined to find success. Since the sun was shining and the temperature was relatively cool for late summer, I decided to walk. My focus for today would be on nearby restaurants.

Many of the places I stopped in took my resume and said they would give me a call if they had any openings come up. By 1 o'clock, my energy started to diminish and I was beginning to get hungry. I remembered seeing a hot dog vending cart when I passed the park, earlier that morning. Considering it was well within budget, I decided to sit there and have lunch.

The park was a decent size for being in the city. There were many beautiful tree-lined paths to run or walk on. I was surprised by how busy it was for a Monday afternoon. Apparently, the city folks did not take this place for granted. I noticed a few other people, dressed in their fancy office clothes, scattered about eating their own lunch, so I found a bench to sit down.

The sun crept behind the clouds and the air was much warmer and thicker than it had been earlier, foreshadowing a good chance for rain. I removed the foil wrap around my hot dog and took a bite. *Not bad, considering it came from a vending cart!* I thought to myself, when all of a sudden, a giant gray dog with pointed ears came charging up at me. He jumped across my lap and stole my hot dog right out of my hand! I was completely taken aback. Thankfully, I could see there was a leash attached to his collar.

"No Lucas! No!" I heard a voice shouting from a few feet away. "Oh my God, I'm so sorry! Christ! Are you okay?" He asked as I watched

Lucas make quick work of devouring my hot dog.

"Don't worry, he may be rude, but he's also harmless. He's just a puppy... we're still working on his manners, aren't we, Lucas?" The guy said to me as he caught with his dog and me.

"A puppy?! Your dog is as tall as I am!" I said, turning to see an athletically fit looking guy who appeared to be in his late twenties. He stood around six feet tall and was wearing a large loose fitting blue tank top, gray sweatpants and black sneakers. He had dark wavy brown hair that was short in the back and long in the front. When he tucked a strand of hair away from his face to reveal his gorgeous light blue eyes, I immediately began to blush. He looked oddly familiar to me, but I couldn't put my finger on it. *Did I know this guy from somewhere? No, I just got to Boston a few days ago.* I quickly reminded myself.

He extended his hand out to shake my own. Instantly, I felt a tinge of what can best be described as the static you get when you rub a balloon on your head and your hair sticks up. "Hi, I'm Jasper." He said, wrapping the leash around his other hand twice to get a better hold of it.

"Carla," I said, shaking his hand, awkwardly, while my brain tried its best to process this strange feeling I had.

This guy was so attractive, I started to feel extremely nervous, but in a good, butterflies in the stomach sort of way. My heart began to flutter as it played "skip to the loo" within each beat.

"Nice to meet you... Carla!" He said, looking at me strangely. *Had he*

57

recognized me too? Or maybe he felt that same strange static feeling I did? I was certainly too shy to ask him.

"Uh… well, why don't we go get you another hot dog, my treat!" He offered, breaking the awkward silence.

"Oh… that's not necessary." I said. I don't know what came over me, but it sure wasn't hunger for a hot dog.

"Nonsense! It's the least that I can do." He said. "Besides, you barely ate any of it…. We won't bite, err, again, I promise!" He laughed, realizing that Lucas did technically eat the hot dog straight out of my hand. By now, Lucas moved on from the hot dog, and started licking me all over my face.

"Down, Lucas! Down!" Jasper shouted, pulling at Lucas's leash.

I couldn't help but laugh, which helped put the tension of my nerves at ease. It was enough to agree to go with them. Besides, there were plenty of other people in the park, God forbid of anything, and the vending cart wasn't very far away. *Was it odd that I actually felt safe in their presence, already anyway?* I wondered. *Well, despite the shocking hot dog attack, that is.*

~

"So… what kind of dog is Lucas?" I asked while we were walking.

"He's a Great Dane mix. I got him from the rescue shelter. I volunteer there sometimes. Clearly, we still have some training to do." He laughed, as Lucas circled around us nearly tripping us both.

"Aww, well that's very sweet," I said, while graciously trying to regain my balance. "Do you know how old he is?"

"They say he's somewhere around five months old. His paws are huge, so he still has some growing to do. Apparently not many people have the space for such a large dog here in the city. After being in the shelter for nearly three months, Lucas was in cue to be euthanized. I just couldn't see him go down like that. And well, here we are now getting ourselves into all sorts of trouble, now aren't we Lucas?" Jasper said with a wink in Lucas's direction.

"Well, if it makes you feel any better, I have always been a magnet for dogs. Especially the big dumb ones." I laughed. "I used to have a boxer mixed breed named Harley when I was growing up. She followed me home one day while I was at the park with my friends. I swear, that dog followed me everywhere I went! I was so sad when she passed away." I said. The mere mention of Harley brought me a sea of mixed emotions. Both happy and sad.

"Oh, I'm sorry to hear that. It's never easy to lose a pet." Jasper said, consolingly.

"Eventually Mama got us a new dog to help me feel better about losing Harley. There's a big difference between a boxer and a chihuahua though." I laughed. "Harley would easily take up more than half my bed, while Crystal could curl herself up so small, you could barely tell she was there most of the time. Crystal was also very attached to me. She's still alive, Mama still has her now."

"Well, I'm not surprised at all, dogs make great judges of character." The way Jasper's face lit up when he smiled really did a number on me, inside. I didn't want to let him in on how much he was affecting me, so when we reached the hot dog stand, I was thankful for the distraction.

"So, how do you take your hot dog?" Jasper asked.

"Spicy mustard and extra sauerkraut, drained please." I replied.

"Great! We'll take two of those, please and two cokes" Jasper told the vendor as he reached into the pocket of his sweats to grab his wallet. He pulled out a twenty dollar bill and told him to keep the change, leaving the vendor with a twelve dollar tip. *That was nice.* I had a deep respect for good tippers. Most of my work experience was spent in the service industry, except for that one job I took doing data entry in an office. I loved the data entry job, unfortunately, it was only a temporary position that ended after three months.

We stopped at a bench to sit down and eat. Just as I was taking a bite of my hot dog, we heard a loud roar of thunder and a moment later, it started raining pretty hard. *What was it about these dang hot dogs?* I wondered as we both ran for cover under a big shade tree nearby, with Lucas in tow. The three of us were soaked! To my horror, the rain had washed away my makeup, revealing the bruise over my eye I had tried to cover up.

"Hey, what happened to your eye?" He asked, looking deeply concerned. I felt so embarrassed. I honestly didn't know what to tell him. All I could think of was to make something up.

"Uh... I fell out of bed the other night and hit the corner of the nightstand." I replied, my nerves, smacking me in the face with guilt for lying. *I hated lying!* I could feel my face turning crimson red, so I did the only thing I could think of. *Run!*

"I'm so sorry, I gotta go!" I said, turning towards the direction of Jamie's apartment.

"Wait! Where are you going?" Jasper shouted out after me.

I didn't want to be rude. "It was nice to meet you, Jasper! Thanks so much for the hot dog!" I shouted back into the rain and kept on running as if my life depended on it.

I didn't care that it was nearly monsooning. I could easily grab a shower when I got back to the apartment which was only about ten minutes away. I kept on running and never looked back.

It felt so strange, on one hand, I was reeling from the whirlwind of emotions enveloping me from my strange encounter with Jasper, but on the other hand, I felt so embarrassed. I was fairly certain he didn't buy my story about the bruise above my eye.

We never exchanged numbers or anything, so at least I wouldn't have to deal with it, but the truth was, there was something very peculiar about this guy. I could almost feel a sense of longing to see him again.

Chapter 14

❧

Jamie finally made it home around 6 o'clock. Hanging out in her apartment by myself did feel a little strange. Even though I had always cherished my time to be alone, I still wasn't used to having it in *her* apartment.

Although the temptation to tell her about what happened at the park was evident, I typically kept things to myself before blurting them out to the people I know, including my best friend. I found the mystery of everything rather intriguing as my imagination drew up scenarios in a tantalizing treat. Having been called a daydreamer countless times by my teachers, I couldn't rebut, it was for good reason.

"Hey Jamie. How was school?" I asked as I watched Jamie take her shoes off and plop herself down on the couch next to me.

"I had an amazing day! Guess who texted me this afternoon?" She asked. This was a great example of how she and I differed. She didn't waste any time in telling me all about what was going on with her in *her* life. Straight, blunt and to the point, that was Jamie. I had always been thrilled to learn about everything that mattered to her, whereas she often had to draw my secrets out of me.

"Hmm... I know, it was Felix, your first boyfriend. He called to tell you he never stopped loving you-that he could never find anyone else to fill the void in his life since the two of you broke up in junior high. And I'm guessing he now wants you guys to elope in Las Vegas? Am I right?" I teased her and we both laughed.

"Felix? I remember him!" Jamie giggled. "Talk about a blast from the past! Wow... Someone's in her creative spirits, today! Maybe I should be asking how *your* day went, hmm?!" She retorted.

Admittedly, she did have good intuition, despite my efforts of keeping my secrecy. I still hadn't decided to divulge, however, so I threw the attention back to her where it belonged in the first place.

"So who was it that texted you, really? Was it Dillon, the cute yellow shirt guy from the club?" I asked. As it turns out, I guess I wasn't so bad at diversions either.

"Indeed, it was! We actually met for coffee before I came home. He really is a hottie, isn't he?" she said, sighing to herself.

Jamie wasn't googly eyed about guys very easily, I could easily tell this guy was special to her.

"Really? So that's where you've been?" I said. "Aww, well I am happy for you! So... How did it go?" I asked, curiously.

"It went well... really well." She replied, smiling from ear to ear. "We made plans to 'make plans' this weekend. He asked how you were doing by the way. I told him it was sweet of him to ask and that you were feeling much better. "

"I can totally tell you like him," I said. "You are absolutely glowing, Jamie. Give me all the details!" *Selfish!* Here I was demanding everything from Jamie, and giving absolutely nothing in return. I snickered silently at my own self critique.

"I think I really do like him. He's a real estate investor. He actually lives in Long Island and is planning on being here for two weeks. He did say, however, that he comes up here often for work and to see his friend, Eddie who lives here. It definitely seems workable for me, especially with everything I have going on with school and work. Enough about me, though, it's your turn to spill the beans," she said. "How did your job hunting go, today?" *Ahh, yes!* This was information I *was* willing to let go of. I could give her that, at the very least.

"Well, let's just say that many restaurants know I'm available, but no bites as of yet. I wasn't able to get to them all though. It started raining and I got soaked!" I said, while noting how hindsight always seemed funnier than when things happen in the moment, as I recalled how much water I wrung out of Jamie's blouse before tossing it into the laundry. "By the way, we may need to print out my resumes again for tomorrow. I must have lost the folder you gave me. I'm sorry." I said, apologetically.

"No worries, it's no trouble at all. I've got plenty of folders, paper and ink. Whatever it takes, we're gonna find you something, for sure!" She said while picking up her laptop from the dining room table.

I had to appreciate her positive attitude towards me. It seemed so long since I felt supported in anything I did. Feeling grateful, I offered to cook us some dinner so Jamie could take a shower and relax

~

"Chicken Parmesan with Fettuccine Alfredo? A girl could really get used to this!" Jamie said, taking her first bite. "Mmm, so good!"

"Thanks, I'm glad you like it. I'm also glad you enjoy cooking as much as I do. Everything I needed to make it was readily on hand. I'll be sure to hand your compliments over to the chef!" I said, patting myself on the back. Jamie laughed at my display of dramatics.

I had to agree. So far, our living arrangements seemed to be working out pretty complimentary. After dinner, Jamie resorted to her bedroom to study and I watched movies on the couch. I was looking forward to getting out to pound the pavement again the following day, so I went to bed a little early.

In hopes of somehow recreating another rendezvous with Jasper and his adorably giant sized pup, Lucas., I had already planned on having lunch at the park. It was silly of me to rely on the fact that he might be a creature of habit, thinking he might take Lucas out to the same spot at exactly the same time every day, but a girl could dream, right?

Chapter 15

The next morning, as planned, I began plastering my resume all over town. Still no definite bites. I was in need of a little pick me up, so I stopped in at the little coffee shop located inside the corner bookstore across from the park. After waiting in line for nearly fifteen minutes, I figured it might be a good idea to grab an application in case they might be hiring. I hadn't thought of working at a coffee shop, but they did appear to be understaffed compared to their business needs.

"How can I help you?" The girl behind the counter asked, while tucking an invasive curl beneath her visor cap. She looked frazzled, like she'd had a really rough day.

"Can I have a coffee with milk and Splenda?" I said, taking note of the delicious looking pastries on display. "I'll also have a chocolate croissant. Can you warm it up, please?" I asked. The girl looked annoyed. I felt bad, but I was far too hungry to let it sway my decision to eat. "By the way, are you guys hiring by any chance?" I asked, trying not to be too much of an inconvenience.

"Ben!" She called out to a guy who must've been lost somewhere behind the scenes. "Grab this girl an application please!"

A moment later, Ben appeared with the application in his hand. He was tall, clean shaven and had curly light brown hair. I couldn't help but think he'd been hiding from the crowd.

"When can you start?" *Hmm... Was that a hint of desperation in his tone?* I wondered.

"Would tomorrow work?" I asked, trying not to sound too excited.

"Tomorrow, then!" He said. "Here, fill this out and bring it back to me this afternoon before 3 o'clock! I assume you have an ID and social security card, right? Bring those with you!" He said.

"Thank you," I said. I took the application from his hands and watched him scurry back to his office. By then, my order was ready. I handed the girl a five dollar tip and thanked her for my coffee and croissant. It wasn't much, but it was still a decent tip. I could already see the sparkle return to her eyes as she thanked me. I knew all too well how good it felt to feel appreciated for working hard.

I took the application with me and headed over to the park to fill it out. I was thrilled to have something solid to tell Jamie about. I wasn't sure about all the details of the job yet, but I was excited to know, I now had an opportunity to make some money. This was definitely a start, at the very least.

The park wasn't as busy today, as it was the day before. Up ahead, I could see the hot dog stand, and suddenly began to feel that butterfly sensation in the pit of my stomach again. I waved hello to the vendor as I passed by and he waved back at me.

I took a seat on the bench where I met Jasper and carefully filled out the application from the coffee shop. The croissant was so good, I had to vow to myself to ease up after this one. Soon I would be working at the coffee shop, with full access to these heavenly chocolate bites of deliciousness.

Once I finished the application, I hung out for a few more minutes and watched as the people moved about. I could hear the birds singing in the trees. The warm breeze carried the laughter of the children at the playground around the corner. It felt so serene to just sit there and take it all in.

There was no sign, however, of Jasper and Lucas. I knew it was a long shot, but coming here wasn't a total loss. I was beginning to really love this park, anyway, I thought to myself as I stood up to make my way back to the coffee shop to turn in my application. When I arrived, I was happy to see that the line had dissipated.

"It's a part time gig. Pay is minimum wage plus tips. Tips are pooled and divided among whoever works that shift and paid out on the next day. You'll get fifty percent off on food and drinks while you're on the clock and a fifteen percent discount anytime at the bookstore. We open at 6:30 am, so you'll need to be here at 6 AM sharp until 11 AM, sometimes noon if we're still busy, which happens often. Everyone gets one 30 minute break, are we clear?" Ben spat out in what seemed to be one breath. "You'll be taking over Peggy's shifts Tuesday through Friday, since she just had to go out and get herself knocked up by some 'rando' guy she met at a bar! I'll be surprised if he sticks around!" He added, clearly annoyed at Peggy's situation and how it affected him. Widely inappropriate and more information than I needed to know, but who was I to tell *him* that. I laughed to myself. His oversharing did, however, clue me in on Ben's demeanor as my new boss.

"Yes, that sounds great!" I said, keeping my discernment to myself.

"Good! Welcome aboard!" He said with a smile that almost looked forced. I could already tell that he and I were going to get along just fine, so long as I didn't make his job any harder than it had to be. Ben seemed quite dramatic, but also very amusing to me.

"Thank you. So, what should I wear?" I asked, hoping it wouldn't cost me an arm and a leg to buy my uniform.

"Blue Jeans, black tee shirt and comfy black shoes. Be prepared to be on your feet a lot. We provide you with your apron, visor cap and a name tag." He said. "Do you have any other questions for me?"

"No, that'll do for now, thanks! I'll see you tomorrow… bright and early!" I added, with a little more enthusiasm than necessary. And with that, Ben resorted back to his office.

I couldn't wait to tell Jamie about my first job in Boston. I mean, sure, it was only a minimum wage job, but I was counting on the tips to help out a little. It didn't even dawn on me that I could also get a discount on books too. Being the avid reader that I was, this perk turned out to be a huge plus for me.

I left the coffee shop feeling like the day had been productive enough for me to call it a wrap. I decided to head back to Jamie's apartment to lie down and take a little nap before she came home from school.

~

I think Jamie may have been more excited about my job than I was, if that was even possible. I wasn't looking forward to waking up before the crack of dawn, but I was happy to have found something I could do to start earning some money. It definitely had me reeling.

"This is going to be so much fun!" Jamie said. "Now we can both wake up, have our coffee and get ready together in the mornings. Plus, you won't ever have to worry about oversleeping, because I never oversleep. I'll even drag you out of bed if I have to." She insisted.

"Well, it is a start," I said. "but if I do decide to stay here, I will definitely need something that will help generate a little more income."

"Understandable," She agreed. "For now, let's celebrate! I'm taking you out to dinner. Your choice, my treat!"

"You don't have to do that, Jamie, but I know you. Once you get an idea in your head, there's no talking you out of it." I conceded. "Hmm... Are there any good Thai food places around here?" I asked.

"Yes! That sounds perfect, actually. It's been a while since I had Thai food... sounds delicious! We'd probably better get a move on it, though, since you need to get to sleep early tonight."

~

The restaurant was a little further out, so we took Jamie's car. We each decided to have a glass of wine with dinner to commemorate my new job. Jamie ordered coconut curry and I ordered my favorite, Chicken Pad Thai. By the time we got back to Jamie's apartment, my belly was full and I was ready for a shower and bed.

Jamie was right, if I had any chance at getting up before 5 am, an early bed time would only aid in my success. The required attire, thankfully, wasn't a problem with the clothes I had brought with me. I would, however, need to buy a few more black tee shirts and better sneakers once I got paid. It wasn't very long after that thought, that I'd settled myself down enough to drift off to sleep.

Chapter 16

M y first day at the coffee shop went well. Brooke, the same girl who had taken my order on the previous day, was there to greet me in the morning. She trained me in opening up the cafe. She looked to be a few years younger than me. Just over five feet tall, Brooke had shoulder length, curly dark brown hair, with golden highlights. She was proportionately curvy and her caramel colored skin complimented her beautiful hazel green eyes.

I was honestly shocked at how many different ways there were to make coffee. That portion of training proved to be a little more challenging than I had anticipated. By the end of the day, however, I seemed to be getting the gist of things.

Working in the service industry for quite some time now, one thing I never really had to do was handle customers before they had their morning coffee. Some of them were more grumpy and impatient than others, especially because I was still learning.

The line was non stop all morning. I could easily see why Brooke had appeared so 'over it' when I first saw her. Especially considering she was all by herself. Today, however, she showed a great deal of patience with me as I learned everything. I sensed that she was grateful for the help and she seemed happier to not be alone in the workload. We worked pretty well as a team, and for that, I was very happy.

When Ben arrived at 9 AM, he covered each of our breaks for an hour before resorting to his office for the rest of the day. Brooke seemed very annoyed by his lack of teamwork. In her eyes, a manager was also supposed to step in and help out when business demand called for it. While I did agree with her, I had previous experience with Ben's style of management, so I guess I was a little more conditioned to handle it. The workspace behind the counter wasn't very big, I could understand why Ben may have preferred to stay behind the scenes and out of the way. I didn't let that on to Brooke, though. I wanted to ensure she and I got along well enough before voicing any of my opinions.

~

When my shift ended at noon, Ben thanked me and told me I did a great job for my first day. I couldn't see how he would even know, because he was barely out in the storefront with us the entire day. It was my guess that he based it off of Brooke's attitude. She seemed a whole lot happier and must not have had any complaints about my work ethics when he called her into the office before I left.

Since I didn't have all that much to do with my afternoon, I decided to browse inside the bookstore for a little while before heading home. I was going to take full advantage of my discount and planned to treat myself with a few books once I got my first paycheck.

The bookstore was nearly triple the size of our little cafe space. There were a few lounge areas for folks who preferred to relax and hang out. I selected a few books and found a comfortable chair to sit and read the blurbs to help me decide which ones I wanted to buy, when my phone started to buzz inside my pocket.

Unknown Caller:

DO YOU LIKE SURPRISES?

Me:

Who is this?

Unknown Caller:

... YOU FIRST

Me:

I don't understand. Do I Know you? I just got this number, I don't have your number saved in my phone.

Unknown Caller:

I'M SO SORRY. I HAVE TO GO. I'LL TEXT YOU AGAIN LATER.

That was the last text I received from the unknown caller. The mystery behind it was very odd to me. *Who the hell could this be? Was it AJ? Did he get a hold of my new number, somehow?* I can almost bet that he would be furious with me for leaving the way that I did. *How would he have gotten this number though?* I pondered.

The only people I had given my new number out to were Jamie, My mom and Ben, my new manager. Oh and several different restaurants I had applied to.

I had no doubt that neither my mom nor Jamie would have sent me texts like this, and I just left Ben who was right across the bookstore. *Could it be a job offer?* If so, it would be an uncanny way to scout out a potential employee, I thought.

I placed the books back on the shelves and started to make my way home. I was tempted to stop in at the park as I passed by, when it started to thunder. Looking up into the sky, I could see the cloud formation had definitely turned ominous and the wind was beginning to pick up. It was inevitably going to rain soon, so instead I headed back to Jamie's apartment. It was the perfect weather for an afternoon nap, which was becoming a trend I could only welcome.

I had to pick up my pace as I raced the clouds to Jamie's apartment. Relief washed over me when I arrived without getting soaked. Just as I was typing in the pin for the elevator, the security officer called out to me.

"Miss Carla?" He asked, eyeing me curiously.

How does he know my name? Did Jamie tell him? Was I in some sort of trouble for not being on the lease? Reluctantly, I turned to face the attractive older gentleman, with kind eyes and a silver beard. It was my guess that he was in his early fifties. I couldn't help but wonder. *What on earth could he be calling me for?*

"Yes, that's me." I said in a cautious tone.

"These came for you today. Since no one was home, the courier was instructed to hand them to me for you" He said, while handing me a beautiful arrangement of gardenias set inside a crystal vase. Gardenias were my favorite flowers.

"They did?" I asked. I was honestly shocked.

"Yes, but I don't see a card attached." He said. I carefully took the crystal vase from his hands.

"They're beautiful, just like you." He said with a wink and a smile. *Charming*, I thought.

"That's very nice of you to say. Thank you, Charlie." I smiled back at him. At least *he* was wearing a name tag, and there would be no mystery to where I'd gotten his name from.

Today sure was full of surprises. First the strange text message from some mysterious unknown caller who literally asked me if I liked surprises. Then there was the security guard, Charlie, who somehow knew me by name. Come to think of it, I suppose he could have learned it from the courier. And now some other mysterious person was sending me gardenias! Of all the flowers they could have sent, they must have known these were my favorite! I wasn't complaining, honestly. There were only a few people who even knew that gardenias were my favorite. My Mom, my sister, Abby, Jamie and AJ, who never seemed to care enough to buy them for me, even when things had been going well between us.

I placed the vase on the dining room table and took in their fragrance. It was why I loved them so much as they smelled just as beautiful as they were. I wondered why here was no card attached. *Was there some hidden message that wasn't being told?*

My head was swirling with so many thoughts as I tucked myself into bed. I had a thousand questions. If I could somehow figure out who it was, then maybe I could find out why they'd sent them to me or vice versa. Most of all, I think it was important to find out *who* it was that sent them.

If it was AJ, how the hell did he find me? Should I be fearful because he was angry that I left the way I did? Was it a message telling me that he knows where I am, and I should watch my back? Or on the other hand, maybe he was feeling remorseful for his behavior and was trying to win me back? My brain was getting dizzy with all the possible scenarios..

I still didn't know how I felt about the idea of going back to live with AJ. My instincts were telling me it was truly over between us, but my heart had no interest in hearing or accepting what my gut had to say about it. I was honestly exhausted just thinking about it. I let the roaring of the thunder and the rain slamming against the window convince me to try to let it go and just relax. Before long, I had fallen into a deep sleep.

Chapter 17

"Carla, honey, wake up!" Jamie was shaking me. My eyes flew open.

"Jamie?" I rubbed my eyes. They were wet from tears.

"I think you were having a nightmare. You were crying and muttering something in your sleep, but I couldn't make out what you were saying. Are you okay?"

It took me a minute to come to my senses. If I had been dreaming, I couldn't recall what it was I was dreaming about.

"I, I don't know what I was dreaming about." I replied.

"Well as long as you're OK," she said. "But you certainly didn't seem OK, so I hope you don't mind that I woke you up." She looked worried.

"Not at all. I didn't intend on sleeping this long, anyway" I said, glancing up at the clock on the wall.

"OK. Where did you buy those flowers from? They're so pretty!" she asked. *Well, that crosses her name off the list of suspects*, I thought.

"Oh my God, Jamie, I have so much to tell you." I cried, suddenly recalling the morning I had. There was no way I was keeping all of this to myself.

I told Jamie everything that had occurred that morning. She found it amusing and suspected I might have a secret admirer on my hands. I sincerely doubted it. I barely knew anyone in this city.

"That's not possible! I've only been here for three days." I asked, not buying her suspicion.

"Well, if it is AJ, how do you think he would have found you so quickly?" she asked.

"Well, he knows you live in Boston, but three days? That's awfully quick to have found me, especially since he did everything to make me run in the first place."

"You're right," she said. "Maybe we should go get a restraining order." Her expression told me she was far from kidding.

"Wait... Let's not jump to any conclusions," I wasn't mentally prepared to get that ball rolling just yet. "I honestly doubt AJ is that resourceful. Especially not while he's drinking the way he has been."

I couldn't help but wonder if his anger with me for leaving could somehow drive him sober enough to come find me. I decided not to enlighten Jamie with that suggestion. I didn't want to encourage her any further on the restraining order idea.

"You're probably right," she said. "Just to be safe, though, we should get you some mace. Or better yet, maybe we can take some self defense classes. I saw a flier posted at the gym just a few days ago. I'll see if we can still sign up!" She offered.

"I suppose it couldn't hurt," I said. I can certainly agree to those measures, especially if it helps to put her mind at ease and lets me off the hook of filing a police report. A part of me still felt remorseful for leaving AJ. I didn't want him to actually get arrested. If the police learned about everything he'd put me through, he would probably even get jail time.

"It's settled then, I will sign us both up for classes tomorrow morning when I go to the gym before school. I think I may have some pepper spray in one of my old purses. I'm going to find it for you to carry with you whenever you leave the house. By the way, my membership at my gym allows me to bring a buddy, so you're welcome to come with me anytime."

"Deal." I said. "I suppose I could come with you on the days that I'm off, which are Saturday, Sunday and Monday, by the way if I hadn't told you."

"That's good, I'm pretty sure they have an early class on Monday mornings. I actually thought about checking it out, myself, before you came here. I guess now is a better time than any." She said.

Jamie always kept herself in good shape. We both had memberships at our local gym before she left for Boston. Finding her motivation admirable, I had only put around half the time that she did into exercising.

We decided to have dinner at home. Jamie made tacos for Taco Tuesday and in true fashion, she chose Fatal Attraction for our dinner feature. Once the movie was over, Jamie went to work in her bedroom. She held a part time position doing research for a local law firm as part of her internship. While I, on the other hand, decided to keep myself parked on the couch and watched Uncle Buck in an attempt to lighten things up a bit before heading to bed, myself.

Chapter 18

Ｍy second day of work at the coffee shop flew by. We were busy all morning long. In my opinion, Brooke and I seemed to team up pretty well. Our tip box appeared to be twice as full as the day before. *Cha-Ching!*

Ben didn't show up until 9:30 and Brooke was furious! He covered our breaks and went back inside his office. I couldn't help but wonder if he was actually working back there. I mean, surely he had to have some official work to do, like ordering supplies and what not, right? I told Brooke to go ahead and take her break first since she clearly seemed upset that Ben was late.

I wasn't sure if I was imagining things, but I could have sworn I saw a dog pass by the window of the coffee shop that resembled Lucas. I tried my best to see if it was Jasper behind him but we were so busy and Brooke was on break, so Ben was working side by side with me. The last thing I needed was to get myself in trouble on my second day for not focusing on the customers. *Damn it!* It wasn't like I was ballsy enough to go outside chasing after him, anyway. No, it would have to look unintentional and organic, as if we just bumped into each other in order for me to even consider making any kind of move.

Caught in my daydream, Ben nudged me on my shoulder to look up at the customer. She'd been standing in front of me trying to place her order while I was lost in la la land. *So much for staying focused.* I laughed to myself. Thankfully, Ben didn't make much of it.

When Brooke returned, I made myself a breakfast sandwich and a coffee to take with me, figuring I could eat my breakfast at the park. *Maybe Jasper and I might cross paths again.* That's if he was even at the park. *I mean, how many giant gray dogs were there in this city, really?*

Am I obsessing? I wondered as I sat down at *our* bench. *Why was I so drawn to a guy I had barely spent more than five minutes with, anyway?* It was silly, but here I was, sitting on a park bench hoping he might pass by me again. *No such luck!*

When my break was over, I walked back to the coffee shop. I was being ridiculous, anyway. I needed to let it go. After all, if we were meant to meet again, the universe would certainly provide the time and space for it to happen naturally, as it had the first time we met.

When my shift was over, Ben called me back into his office. *Uh oh!* Surely, he would scold me for daydreaming in front of the customers. To my surprise, he handed me an envelope instead.

"What's this?" I asked, taking the envelope from his hands.

"If you don't want it, I'll gladly keep it!" he joked. "That's your share of tips from yesterday, silly girl."

"Oh! Thanks Ben!" I giggled, while tucking the envelope into the outside pocket of my purse.

"Don't thank me, thank yourself, honey! You're the one who earned it! Great work by the way!" He added, softening his tone.

I got the feeling, he was well aware of just how callous he could be at times. I could see my instincts about Ben were already beginning to take shape. Certainly there was a nice person, underneath the forefront.

I waited until I came home to check and see how much cash was in the envelope. In my years of waiting tables, I always waited until the guest was gone before returning to take my tip off the table. It always felt awkward to pick it up in front of them. I thoroughly enjoyed the anticipation of seeing how much my service was worth, though.

Twenty-six dollars? Hey, not bad for my first day working a six hour shift at a coffee shop, I thought. This would increase my pay to four dollars more per hour. Obviously twenty-six dollars wasn't going to go very far, but I was pleased to see I could earn at least another hundred dollars on top of my paycheck. That would put me somewhere around the same income, working full time at the grocery store.

I had always enjoyed working and feeling useful to others. Mostly because I could care for my own needs, independently. Some might call me a people -pleaser, I call it having a passion for the service industry.

Even though it had been a while since I genuinely felt happy on the inside, people would always compliment me on my smile. I made it my daily mission to turn every frown I encountered upside down. It had brought me joy to help other people who were sad inside, to smile too. Smiling became second nature to me and I think it also may have helped me keep a seed of contentment, at least to some degree. In the face of the sadness I felt, while living with AJ, working had sort of become my own escape from reality.

The moment I set my phone down on the charger, it began to vibrate.

Mama:

Hi Baby. How are things? Are you still in Boston?

I'm pretty sure I had conditioned my own mother to text me, rather than call, since I never answered her calls anymore, either. I always returned her calls by text, so she would at least know that I was alive. It wasn't that I didn't like talking to her, I just knew that if I had spoken to her directly, she would be able to sniff out that things weren't all okay with me.

Me:

Hi Mama! Yes, I'm still in Boston. Things are going great! Thanks for asking. I'll call you a little later, I have lots to tell you!

My circadian rhythm must have grown accustomed to my afternoon naps because I was already growing tired. *Well, that didn't take very long, now did it?* I thought to myself.

Mama:

That sounds wonderful, dear. I would love to hear all about it. By the way, I ran into Amber at the grocery store yesterday. I told her you were up in Boston with Jamie. She told me to tell you to give her a call when you can.

Me:

Okay, I will, thanks for the message!

Mama:

You're welcome, honey. Talk soon! Love you!

Me:

Love you too, Mama <3

I was just about to doze off when my phone rang. I grabbed it off the nightstand to find the caller ID read UNKNOWN CALLER. For a moment I was frozen, downright petrified. My first instincts whispered to me that it could have been AJ. A good part of me really wanted to pick it up just so I could finally figure out who the hell it was, but my anxiety got the best of me.

I had no doubt in my mind, I was far from ready to have any communication with AJ, so I just let it ring. After six rings and what seemed an eternity, the ringing finally stopped. *Thank God.* I really hoped that whoever it was would've decided to leave me a message on my voicemail. At least, I had hoped they would so I could finally figure out who it was. I was too chicken to find out now anyway, so I pulled the covers up over my head and let my eyes close.

Chapter 19

I woke up a little after 3 o'clock. The apartment was quiet, just as still as it had been when I first laid down. I got out of bed and went into the kitchen to turn on the kettle to make myself some hot tea. I literally jumped out of my skin when I heard my phone ringing from the nightstand in the bedroom. *Sheesh!* This Unknown Caller bit was really making me antsy. I was relieved, however, to find that this time it was only Jamie. *Phew!*

She was calling to let me know that she was meeting Dillon for coffee after school again and asked me if I would mind if she invited him over for dinner, tonight. Of course, I reminded her that it was her apartment and she didn't ever have to ask for my permission. I told her I was excited to meet him, officially, not on the dance floor in the midst of a full fledged panic attack.

After we hung up, I checked my phone to see if the Unknown Caller had ever left a voicemail earlier this afternoon, but there were no messages. *Damn it!* This only added more to the mystery. It was beginning to drive me a little crazy. I thought it might help if I went for a walk to help me take my mind off of it. Perhaps I could find us a bottle of wine to have with dinner. I wasn't sure what Jamie was planning on cooking. I noticed she had taken some ground beef out of the freezer to defrost. Since we both loved red wine, I figured I couldn't go wrong with that. I just had to keep my fingers crossed that Dillon would like it too.

The walk up to the corner store did help to settle my nerves, thankfully. I was happy to find a decent bottle of Cabernet Sauvignon on sale. *Perfect!* I thought, as I grabbed it off of the shelf and proceeded to the checkout counter. I was really growing fond of how convenient everything was here, in Boston. A trip like this would have easily been a forty minute car ride back and forth, at home, in Wakefield. Whereas, here, I could simply walk to the corner store and be back in less than half the time. Surprisingly, city life was really beginning to grow on me.

~

It wasn't very long after I came home that Jamie made her appearance through the front door. Apparently her dinner invitation had been accepted, because Dillon was trailing behind her carrying a large paper bag full of groceries.

"Hey Carla, this is Dillon. Dillon, this is my oldest and dearest friend Carla. You remember her from the night we met at the club, right?" Jamie said, as she introduced us, formerly.

I could feel my face turning warm. Surely, I was blushing from embarrassment that he might remember how awkward I had been that night.

88

"Pleasure to meet you, Carla." He said, extending his hand out to shake mine.

"You as well." I replied, trying my best to keep my cool. He was very handsome, and spot on for Jamie's type.

"I hope you don't mind, but I will be taking over your kitchen after dinner. I'm going to prepare my famous Strawberry Hazelnut Shortcake for dessert." He said, flashing a quick grin in Jamie's direction.

"That sounds heavenly!" I said. "I don't mind at all! I'm guessing Jamie may have already hinted, the secret to winning my 'BFF seal of approval' can be achieved easily through yummy treats" We all laughed. Jamie was well aware of my love affair with food. I was grateful to feel the energy make a shift into a more relaxing tone as I let the tension in my body melt away.

"Oh, by the way, Jamie, I wasn't sure what you were planning to cook, but I went to the store earlier and got us a bottle of red wine to have with dinner." I added.

"Perfect! That sounds wonderful! Thank you. We're having Rigatoni Bolognese with Spinach."

"That sounds Amazing! How about I help you make dinner?" Dillon offered.

"Done deal! I'll put everything away and get that bottle poppin' " Jamie replied, as she danced her way into the kitchen with the grocery bag.

"I know…. Why don't you give Dillon a quick tour of the apartment while I pour us each a glass of wine, then we can all sit out on the balcony for a bit before we cook dinner." She suggested, calling out from the kitchen. We could hear her fumbling around in one of the drawers.

"Aha! I knew it was in here!" She cried, holding up the old fashioned wine key she must have been looking for.

As requested, I showed Dillon around the apartment. Though he didn't say all that much to me, he did seem pleased with how Jamie decorated her apartment. He stopped to admire some of the artwork on the walls. Afterwards, we met Jamie outside on the patio.

The sky revealed a setting sun, beautifully dressed in a pinkish orange hue that even the hardest of hearts could only admire. Jamie had to have known how breathtaking the view would be at sunset.

"Wow! This view is amazing!" Dillon said, while glancing at Jamie with a twinkle in his eye. I could see the sparks between them were flying high.

"That's what I said when I first saw it, too. Just Incredible!" I agreed. "Perhaps I should let you two hang here for a little bit while I go set the table for us." I had a sneaky suspicion they would probably enjoy the view a little more by themselves.

After carefully arranging each setting, I couldn't help but notice the beautiful touch my gardenias brought to the table. Alive, perky and fragrant as ever, as if they knew we had company over. As I breathed in their essence, the realization crossed over me that I still hadn't figured out who sent them to me. My mind was completely boggled. I took another sip of wine and headed back out to the balcony.

Just as I imagined, Jamie and Dillon were sitting, very cozy together in one of the lounge chairs, deeply locked in a passionate kiss. I cleared my throat and closed the sliding glass door behind me. They both jumped.

"Eh, sorry. I didn't mean to interrupt," I said. I was beginning to feel out of place.

"It's totally fine," Jamie said as she gently broke free from Dillon's embrace. I could sense she didn't want me to feel like I was a third wheel.

"Yeah, why don't we go get dinner started, huh?" Dillon asked.

"Good idea, I am getting hungry." Jamie replied.

"Why don't you two go? I'll stay out here and watch the sun set for a little while longer. That's if you guys don't mind?" I asked, as I took a seat on the other lounge chair.

"Not at all," Jamie said as she and Dillon each stood up to go inside.

Dinner was phenomenal. We learned that Dillon owned a successful real estate company in the tri-state area, with occasional business in Massachusetts and Pennsylvania. He had an older brother, Gary, who was a policeman. He was married with two children. His younger sister, Jessica was a freshman in college. They both lived in New York. Dillon's father had passed away a few years ago, and his mother lived in New Jersey.

We also learned that Eddie happened to be a good friend of his. He was the guy I was dancing with at the club, who unintentionally sent me into a full fledged panic attack. Apparently Eddie asked Dillon to put in a good word for him.

"How would you feel about going out on a double date?" Dillon asked me.

"I don't think Carla's ready to date anyone just yet, she just got out of a relationship." Jamie offered, as she came to my rescue.

"Jamie's right, I think perhaps we should wait a little while on that one," I laughed, "But I will tell you one thing I am ready for... That decadent dessert you promised us." I said, smacking my lips.

"You got it! Coming right up! You two sit right here, I got this!" He said, excusing himself from the dinner table. Jamie and I both watched as he scurried off into the kitchen.

"Well, what do you think?" Jamie whispered quietly so Dillon couldn't hear us.

"So far, he seems perfect!" I whispered back and gave her two thumbs up.

A few minutes later, Dillon appeared with two plates. He set one down in front of Jamie and the other in front of me, then went back into the kitchen to get his own plate. "OK ladies, prepare yourselves. I may or may not have gotten a marriage proposal after this one."

Jamie and I looked at each other and at our plates and we each grabbed our forks.

"To be fair, I should also admit she was my mother's friend and a good twenty-five years older than me." He laughed.

Of course, I was the first to dig in. "Oh my God... How does this taste even better than it looks?!"

"I took the liberty of getting the dairy free whipped cream. Jamie mentioned you were allergic, so don't worry about that." he said.

"That's very thoughtful of you both. Thank you!" I said. "Yep, this seals the deal, Dillon. You have officially passed my 'BFF seal of approval' test with flying colors!" I said, with mouthful of strawberries and cream. They both smiled.

After finishing my dessert, I pretended to yawn, giving myself an exit in the event that Jamie might want to spend some time alone with Dillon. I certainly didn't want to stand in the way of her love life. It was getting late anyway, and I did have to get up early in the morning.

"Well guys, I think I'm going to turn in for the night, it was so nice to meet you Dillon. We should definitely do this again soon." I said.

"The pleasure was all mine," he insisted, as he stood up from the table to shake my hand.

Chapter 20

~◈~

As I lay in bed, I recounted on how much of a gentleman Dillon seemed to be. He was handsome, charming, thoughtful and very well mannered. Literally checking off all the boxes, he appeared to be a perfect match for Jamie. She truly deserved to be with someone who would treat her well. It was my guess, she just may have found that in Dillon.

The only downfall was that he lived nearly two hours away from Boston. However, I do remember her telling me that he comes here often. With Jamie's schedule, she probably wouldn't have much time to spend with him, even if he did live here. This was honestly the perfect scenario for her current set of circumstances with work and school. I was happy for her. It gave me hope for my own romantic future. I let my contentment carry into my subconscious mind as I drifted off to dreamland.

The grass felt so soft against my bare feet as I made my way down a path into what seemed to be a mystical forest. All of the colors of the trees were vibrant and full of life. Butterflies were swirling all around me and I could feel the warmth of the sun on my skin as I stumbled across a beautiful, glowing river. I could hear the river calling out to me.

I removed the white linen dress I was wearing when I reached the bank and immersed my body into the river. letting the water rush over me. I felt so at peace as I began to swim all around. The temperature of the water could not have been more perfect. I felt so carefree as if there was nothing else in life but this very moment of bliss!

The fish were swimming up to me, greeting their hello's. It was then that I heard a dog barking, somewhere far off in the distance. Curious, I decided to swim towards the sound of the barking. As soon as I got close enough, I could see the silhouette of a man at the other side of the river bank. As his image became clearer, I noticed he was wearing gray sweatpants and a blue tank top. Jasper?

I swam faster as the sense of urgency to get to the other side became stronger than ever. It felt as if I were drawn to him, magnetically. The swarm of butterflies soon began to fly above me. It seemed as though they were magically directing the current to bring me closer towards him, when all of a sudden, my foot got stuck on a root. Whatever it was, was beginning to pull me under. I dipped my head under water to try and free myself. It was at this moment, I realized it wasn't a root at all. It was AJ. He was pulling me down, under the water. I couldn't believe it! AJ was literally trying to drown me.

"Help me!" I called out, as I briefly managed to get some air, then down I went again. The barking became louder. "Help!" I cried, and again, I was pulled back down under the water. I struggled to breathe as AJ kept pulling me down, each time harder than the last. He was so much stronger than I was, but I kept on fighting for my life.

I had almost given up when I could feel someone pulling me up, out of the water. It felt like two forces were playing a game of tug of war with my body. The force from above had quickly overpowered the one from below and at last, I could breathe again.

I looked up to find Jasper's beautiful face. I swear, he looked like an angel. He carried me over to the side of the river bank, where Lucas had jumped into the water to greet us. I looked back down in the water and all I could see was AJ's arms stretched out toward me as his body sunk further below into the river. Jasper saved me from drowning, and AJ. I looked into his dreamy eyes and...

"Carla, wake up!" Jamie was nudging me. "You were crying in your sleep again."

As I began to gather my senses, I could hear my alarm going off on my phone. Jamie took it off the charger and turned off the alarm. It was all a dream. I could swear, It all felt so real.

"Coffee is ready," she said. "You'd better get up, sleepy head, it's ten after five!"

"Uh, yeah. Yes. I'm coming. I'll be out in a few minutes." I said, racing to the bathroom to quickly brush my teeth. I splashed some cold water on my face and noticed in my reflection that the bruise over my eye was nearly gone. *Thank God.* While makeup did serve its purpose, I still wasn't a huge fan of wearing it on my face. I pulled my hair up into a messy bun on top of my head and let out a few strands in front. I rushed to pull on some clothes and decided that no one would notice that my socks didn't match if my jeans were covering them. I needed to do some laundry for sure!

I went into the kitchen to grab a cup of coffee and went outside to meet Jamie outside on the patio.

"Did you sleep okay?" She asked.

"Yes, I had the strangest dream-" I said when it occurred to me that I still hadn't mentioned my rendezvous with Jasper at the park to her yet. "I did. How about you? How did things go last night with Dillon?" I asked, poking her in the arm.

"He left about an hour after you went to bed. I'd be lying if I told you we didn't have an epic make out session. He was a real gentleman. When things got hot and heavy between us, he made sure we didn't go too far." I watched as her eyes darted off into the clouds as if she were lost in the memory.

"Were you surprised at all that he was?" I asked curiously.

"Not really. I wanted us to move things over to my bedroom, but ultimately, I agreed with Dillon that we should probably pump the brakes and take things more slowly. I think I really like him, Carla," She paused for a moment. "He loved you, by the way. He was really nervous to meet you on our way here last night. I could really tell he wanted everything to go smoothly."

"Aww, I really liked him too! I thought the two of you seemed perfect for one another. Tell him as long as he continues to bring his yummy treats, he's welcome anytime." I joked.

"Oh, I forgot to tell you last night, I booked us both for the Self Defense classes on Monday morning. It starts at 7:00 am. Looks like we're gonna turn you into an early bird sooner than you think!" She teased.

"That sounds great! Speaking of early birds, I'd better get going if I don't want to be late!" I said as I quickly downed the rest of my coffee and headed off to work.

Chapter 21

I
t was Friday and we were extremely busy in the morning. I was really beginning to get the hang of things. I even had a few of our regular customers' coffee orders ready for them as they approached the counter. The people loved it. Some of them tipped us even more because they felt the service was more personalized.

Countless times I caught myself staring out the window, expecting Jasper and Lucas to pass by. I swear, I could feel the energy in my body surge every time as if they were going to turn the corner at any moment. I swear, I had never met anyone in my life that had this effect on me. It was almost as if our energy had intertwined with each other that day. I just couldn't seem to keep him off my mind.

As business slowed down around 10:30, it gave Brooke and me a chance to talk and get to know each other better. I learned that she had just graduated from high school and was taking a year off, before deciding where she wanted to go to college. She told me about her boyfriend, Jason, whom she'd been dating for eight months. She seemed happy in her relationship. She had an air of confidence about her that appeared to be untouched.

I told her about AJ and how I wound up in Boston. I also mentioned the flowers that had shown up so mysteriously and about the unknown caller that was haunting me. She seemed genuinely intrigued about the situation and was determined to try and help me figure it out. Honestly, it felt good to talk about it with her.

Apparently, I had to wait another week to get my paycheck, but we both made decent tips. I mentioned to Brooke that I was going to treat myself with a new book from the bookstore after our shift ended. As it turned out, she also loved to read, just like me. She came up with an idea that we could each buy a book and share it with each other when we were finished reading so we could both save money. Then we could discuss them after we both read the book. I happily agreed to that deal!

Brooke decided to come along with me to the bookstore. It was nice to have a new friend in town. I was beginning to feel that even though the idea of coming to Boston seemed crazy at first, it was proving to be my best course of action.

I mean, Jamie was usually pretty good at giving me advice. Initially, I felt that she might also be biased. Now that things were beginning to take shape, I was starting to feel better about my decision. I couldn't help but wonder about AJ sometimes, though. The way I just up and left him had me feeling very unsettled, despite the abuse he put me through.

While we were in line at the bookstore, Brooke offered to treat me to lunch at the pizza place Jamie had taken me to, on my first night here.

I, of course, couldn't pass that offer up, so we headed there next. We sat in the booth by the window. Brooke ordered a whole pie so she could bring home the leftovers.

While we were sitting in the booth waiting for our pizza to be ready, something told me to look out the window. This time, there was no mistaking it. There they were, plain as day. Jasper and Lucas walking across the street, making their way over to *our* park. I gasped.

"What is it?" Brooke asked, wondering if I was OK.

"I'm fine. I'm just really hungry." I laughed, disguising the truth.

"Well, that makes two of us! The pizza here is so good." Brooke recanted.

I still hadn't told anyone about Jasper, but I was rather excited to see that he was still going over to *'our park'*. If nothing else, it brought me hope that one day, we might find ourselves a chance to meet again. Silently, I wondered if he might remember our encounter while he was there. *Was he thinking about me as much as I was thinking about him?*

When our pizza arrived at our table, fresh, hot and steamy, my mouth began to water. I let Brooke have dibs on the first slice, after all, she was the one paying. When my phone began to ring from inside my purse, Brooke and I each paused to look at each other. I pulled it out of my purse to see who it was, and sure enough, the caller ID read UNKNOWN CALLER. I set my phone on the middle of the table and stared at it.

"You should answer it!" Brooke said. "You'll never know who it is until you do!"

She was right, but I was too chicken, still. I continued to stare at it until the ringing finally stopped. I picked it up to see if they'd left a message, and it started to ring again, making me jump.

"Here, I'll answer it for you." Brooke said as she reached across the table to take my phone out of my hands. I conceded. *What could it hurt?*

"Hello?"

"It's a lady" She mouthed over to me so the caller wouldn't hear her.

"I'm sorry, she stepped away from her phone for a moment, may I give her a message?" Brooke asked the unknown caller. Hearing only one side of the conversation was driving me insane.

"Yes, I will have her give you a call in a few minutes, let me grab a pen and paper." She said while motioning to me to look for something to write with.

I found a pen and an old receipt inside my purse and handed it to her. I watched as she scribbled down the information she was gathering from the caller.

"OK, great! Thank you." Brooke said as she hung up the phone. She had a big, old, goofy grin on her face.

"So…. that was Maggie from Silver Linings Hope Center. She said she'd received your resume and wants you to call her back about a receptionist position." She said, laughing.

"Wait... What?" I asked, I was so confused. "I only handed my resume out to restaurants. How would she have gotten my resume?"

"I don't know, but it sure seems like lady luck is smiling down on you, so I certainly wouldn't question it!" Brooke remarked.

"You're right.... At least now I know it's not AJ. Thank God!" I said, breathing a sigh of relief. "I'd better give her a call back soon, before she offers the position to someone else."

"I agree! I actually have to get going anyway. Jason is coming over tonight and I have to clean!" she said, while carefully scooping the remaining pizza into the box the waitress had given her. "Do you want to take some home, too?" She offered while gathering her belongings.

"No, you take it, I'm stuffed. Thanks so much for lunch, by the way! It'll be my treat next time." I said.

"Deal." She said as she leaned over to hug me. "Call Maggie, you totally got this, Babe! I can't wait to hear all about it!"

"Thanks!" I shot back, as I stood up to leave.

After spotting Jasper and Lucas through the window, I was planning to head over to the park to try and catch a glimpse of them, but after Maggie's call, I opted to head back to the apartment instead where I could call her back somewhere quiet.

Chapter 22

C harlie, the security officer, called me over again. This time, he handed me a beautiful, high quality navy blue and silver, floral trim wrapped package tied in a lacy, white bow. The gift box felt a little heavy in comparison to its size. I thanked Charlie and took the package upstairs with me, as I took notice, this time, there actually was a card attached.

A day for revelations? I wondered, as I placed the package on the table next to my gardenias. They were sadly now beginning to fade. I decided to wait until Jamie came home to open the package, since I had some very important business to tend to.

I reached inside my pocket and pulled out the receipt with the scribbled number on it. I stared at it for a moment to let myself wonder what Silver Linings could be. The name of the business, alone, piqued my interest. I drew my phone out of my purse and dialed the number. It rang five times before someone finally answered.

"Silver Linings, there is hope, Maggie speaking," Maggie answered.

Her tone was warm and quick. It sounded as if she was distracted by something else.

Grasping onto her tone, I quickly chimed in. "Hi Maggie, My name is Carla Taylor. I received a message to give you a call."

"Carla, Carla... Oh, yes, Carla! Hi, how are you?" I could hear papers ruffling in the background.

"I understand, you have my resume?" I asked, trying to sound professional.

"Yes, yes I do, and the wonderful recommendation letter, too."

Huh? I didn't recall Jamie typing up a recommendation letter. I certainly wasn't going to tell her that, of course, so I played along.

"So, Carla, I know it's last minute. I did try to reach you yesterday, but would you by any chance be able to interview for our front desk receptionist position, this afternoon at say... 4:30?"

I looked at my watch, it was almost 2:30. "Yes, I can do it at 4:30!" I excitedly replied. "Can you give me your address please?" She quickly gave me the address and thanked me for taking the interview on such short notice and we ended the call. I plugged the address into the GPS app on my phone and found it was only about a mile and a half away. Still, I knew I wouldn't want to walk to an interview and show up sweaty and gross, so I figured I'd better move fast and hop in the shower. Since Jamie told me I could borrow her clothes any time until I was able to shop for new ones, I was sure I'd be able to find something interview worthy.

I found a beautiful light gray suit and a Tiffany-blue blouse to add a nice pop of color. I completed the look with a cute pair of black stiletto flats. Jamie was a little taller than I was, but most of her clothes fit me well enough to go unnoticed. After adding a few curls to my hair with Jamie's curling wand, I brushed on some light makeup and lip gloss. I couldn't help but smile at my reflection. With confidence, I headed out the door.

Silver Linings was not on a main street. Thankfully, I left a little early as it wasn't the easiest of places to find and nothing that I expected it to look like.

I pulled into a security gate that was set in the front of a long driveway to a large courtyard. There were two fairly large cream colored mansion homes with dark brown trim, and charming flower boxes adorning the windows. The mansions looked as though they had each stood there for well over a century. Peeking out from behind the houses, I could see a tennis court on one side and a basketball court on the other, which lead me to wonder just how large this property was.

"Hi Carla, you found us!" Maggie called out to me, when she emerged from the front door of the mansion that stood on the left. She was an attractive woman with wavy brown hair just past her shoulders, and warm brown eyes. She appeared to be somewhere in her late forties, around the same age as my mother.

"OK, so we will need to do this fairly quickly. I have one of our residents covering the phones," she said as she took my hand and guided me onto a stone path that led us to a courtyard that was nestled on the rear side of the property. I noticed a fairly large swimming pool equipped with patio style furniture that sat in between the tennis and basketball courts.

There were a few young children playing in the play yard behind the pool area. The grass was green and hedges were all trimmed. The property appeared to be very well maintained for its age.

On the tour of the grounds, Maggie gave me a brief history of Silver Linings and how the company came about. She said it was established in 1977, when the two decrepit old mansions were sold to Wayne and Amy Engelson. They had plans to turn the mansions into shelter homes for families who were in distress from traumatic events. Wayne and Amy were brother and sister, who lost both of their parents to a devastating house fire. They were each rescued from the fire and became orphans of the state as young teenagers. After being split up, the twins were thrown into various homes until they turned eighteen, at which point they were both awarded with the inheritance their parents left them.

Maggie went on to explain the many services, including shelter, counseling and several resources that Silver Linings offered for people who needed them. She also mentioned that the property was purposely meant to be hidden, due to the nature of the business for privacy of its residents. There were people there that came from all sorts of circumstances.

Upon entry through one of the mansions, she showed me the front desk, where the job I would be taking over would mostly occur. I briefly informed her of my previous work experience and that it had mostly come from the service and hospitality industry. I also gave her some insight on the little bit of office experience I did have, which was mostly data entry.

"This is where you'll be spending most of your time." Maggie said, as she pointed to a large antique desk with a multi-switchboard phone. There were many framed photos and thank you cards pinned up all over the place. Most of the furnishings were antique but also very well kept. It appeared as though the owners wanted to keep the integrity of the history within the estate.

"With the start of the new school year, Leila, our receptionist, had to switch back to part time. I normally cover her lunch break. With her change in schedule, I've had to take over for the rest of the work day, which makes it nearly impossible for me to get any of my own work done."

"I see, and what are the hours for the position?" I asked. So far, this job seemed to be a great opportunity for my situation, if only I was able to keep my job at the coffee shop.

"Well, for now, we mostly need someone during the week, from Monday through Friday. You'll mostly be answering the phones from 3 to 6 PM. I am adding on an extra hour, at least for now, to help me get caught up on some light clerical work and reorganizing of our files. We get a lot of our funding through charity, so I'm afraid the most I can offer at this time is $16.50 per hour." She paused for a moment, to gauge my reaction. "We would love to have you join our team, Carla. What do you say?"

She removed her glasses and wiped a bead of sweat from her forehead. "I know it's rather hot and stuffy in here, but we do have someone coming by to fix the air conditioning this evening," She added, as if that would somehow matter in my decision.

I couldn't do the math in my head fast enough, but it sounded like a dream job for me. "Yes! I'll take it!" I said, excitedly.

"Great! Any chance I can get you to start on Monday?" She asked.

"Monday sounds great! Is there any particular dress code?" I asked.

"Office casual. You can wear jeans on Fridays." She replied.

"That sounds perfect. I do have another job, but it won't interfere with this schedule at all." I said.

"Excellent! Welcome aboard, Carla... I would love it if you could come by an hour early, just on Monday, if you're able to. This way I can show you the switchboard and go over some important ground rules, mostly pertaining to our privacy and safety, here at Silver Linings."

"Well, Monday is actually my day off at the coffee shop, so I can definitely make that work for you." I said, reassuring her.

"Great, I'll see you then! Please make sure you bring your driver's license, social security card and a blank check if you want to have your paychecks directly deposited." She added as she walked me out to my car.

~

I could barely contain my excitement. I shot out a text to Brooke when I got back to the apartment.

Me

I got the job, I start Monday afternoon!

Brooke

I had no doubt you'd nail it! Congrats! Can't wait to hear all about it on Tuesday!

Me

Thanks. Have fun tonight with Jason.

Brooke

Thanks. He'll be here any minute. Hopefully we'll actually get to finish the movie this time ;)

Mama was excited to hear her the news when I called her. I wanted to talk to Abby but she was out with her friends again. I promised Mama I would give her a call after work on Monday evening to let her know how everything went. She reminded me about calling Amber before I hung up with her.

I dug my old phone out of my duffle bag to retrieve Amber's number. I added both her and Heather's numbers into my phone. It felt so awkward calling her because I knew that she and Heather had been upset with me for some time now.

Finally settling on the fact that if they were truly my friends, they would eventually understand. The only way for me to know for sure was to keep a line of communication open with them. I typed Amber's number into my phone and pushed send on the call.

After a few rings, Amber picked up. "Hello?"

"Hi, Amber. It's Carla. How are you?" I asked.

"Hey Carla. I'm good. How are you? Did your mom tell you I ran into her at the grocery store the other day?" Amber asked.

"Yes, she did. She made me promise to call you. I'll be honest, I felt really bad about not keeping in touch with you and Heather for so long."

"It's okay. We really miss you. After you left, Tommy moved into your old bedroom to help us out on the rent. He's always hogging up the television with his stupid video games. It's not the same without you here." She whined.

Tommy was Amber's older brother. The two of us took turns having crushes on each other since high school. It was never the right time for us, though, as we'd each had significant others when the other didn't.

"Oh, I thought he was living with his girlfriend Kallie, no?" I asked.

"No, they broke up again. Shocker!" Amber said, sarcastically.

"Oh, jeez. I'm sorry to hear that. I am glad he was able to take my place though. I know I gave you guys a two month notice before I left, but I still felt terrible for leaving without someone to replace me." I said.

"So what are you doing in Boston anyway?" Amber asked, curiously.

"Well, AJ lost his job not long after we moved to Wakefield-" I started to reply.

"What?! That's crazy, they made you guys move up there for nothing?" She asked.

"I know, right? So things sort of spiraled out of control after that with AJ and his drinking, again. We weren't getting along so well, so I left. Just please don't tell him where I am if you happen to see him around town."

"I knew it!" Amber cut in. "I always felt like he wasn't right for you." She was right about that. It was part of the driving force that pulled me away from Amber. She saw through everything I had conveniently let myself be blinded by. Looking back now, it all seemed clear as day. My love for AJ held a strange way of allowing myself to be victimized by default. I wasn't ready to open up and tell her everything, so I kept the ugliest of details to myself.

"Well, that's actually the reason why I told your mom to have you call me. Tommy told me that he saw AJ get kicked out of O'Malley's last week. He was fighting with some guy about a girl who looked a lot like you. He said AJ was plastered and had to be cut off from the bar." O'Malley's was the bar that AJ and his buddies used to hang out at every weekend.

I followed her news with silence, "Carla? Are you there?" Amber asked while I picked my jaw up off the floor to respond.

"So he was there, in town?" I asked.

"Yes, Tommy got the feeling he was here, looking for you. That's why I wasn't so shocked when your mother told me you were in Boston." She replied.

"Oh wow, I didn't know that." I said. "Well, thank you for letting me know."

"Of course! Listen, I have to go, I'm meeting Heather for dinner soon. Please don't be a stranger and keep in touch, will ya?" She asked.

"I will, for sure." I said. "Keep me posted if you happen to see him again, please."

"I will. It was nice to talk to you. I'm gonna save your new number on my phone. I'll talk to you again soon!" She said, ending our call.

A few minutes after my call with Amber, Jamie came home from school. I spared her the details of my call with Amber. I didn't want to cause her to worry. I did, however, tell her all about my interview with Maggie at Silver Linings.

"I'm so happy for you! Wait, does this mean you'll be staying here in Boston?" She asked.

"Well, all I can say is that for now, we'll just have to see how things go. I really want to help pay my fair share, so if I do stay, we will need to work out those details for sure." I replied. Jamie could tell I was being serious.

"Okay, well your first month here will definitely be rent free, and that is absolutely non negotiable. You need a chance to get yourself established and be able to obtain some of the things you'll be needing to stay. In a month or so, we can discuss something that works for both of us. But for now, we are definitely going to celebrate! Ooh, I know… Why don't we start with this gift on the table with your name on it? Where did it come from?" She asked, curiously.

"Oh my gosh, I forgot all about that! Charlie, the security guard from the lobby, handed it to me when I came home earlier. With everything going on, I wanted to wait until you came home to open it." I replied.

"Well, let's see what the card says, shall we?" she said, handing me the gift.

The card was inside a high quality white stock envelope and had my name hand written on the front. I carefully opened it so as to keep everything intact. I had always been that way with cards and gifts. It drove other people crazy, but I loved to delay the anticipation of what might be inside.

Reminded me of you, I couldn't pass it up. I hope you like it.

That was all that was stated inside the card. It wasn't signed by anyone. I was beginning to think whoever was sending me these gifts wanted to remain a secret. With no words to say, I handed Jamie the card so she could read it.

"It's not signed. See, you do have a secret admirer!" She said, beaming with excitement. "Well, go ahead, open the gift! Maybe there will be some sort of clue as to who it might be from inside the box."

I carefully pulled the lacy ribbon off the box and slid my fingers down the side where the tape was so I could remove the beautiful wrapping paper without damaging it. There was a luxurious velvet box that opened from the top. I removed the top of the box to reveal a jumbo sized aromatic candle with a colorful butterfly on the label. A smaller compartment to the box lay underneath the candle holding a choker style brown leather necklace with a multicolored glass spun charm in the shape of a butterfly.

"Oh, wow! What a thoughtful gift! Simple, yet elegant and sweet, just like you. I don't know who this guy is, but I'm pretty sure I like him already!" Jamie proclaimed as she tied the necklace around my neck. "It looks so pretty on you, Carla."

"It really is a beautiful gift, I honestly love it." I said, stepping in front of the mirror. I loved how the sunlight captured all of the colors so beautifully.

"But who on earth could it possibly be from?" I wondered. "I know now that it's not the Unknown Caller who keeps calling my phone. Apparently that was Maggie trying to get a hold of me, which reminds me... Did you by any chance write a recommendation letter to go with my resume?"

"No. I don't know why I didn't think of that, we probably should have. Why?" Jamie looked confused.

"Maggie said she'd gotten my resume along with a beautiful recommendation letter. I honestly wouldn't be surprised if that letter is what landed me this job, considering I really don't have very much office experience. And I'd only handed my resume out to about a dozen restaurants. It's so bizarre, isn't it? I don't even know how she got my resume in the first place." I said.

"Maybe one of the restaurants forwarded it to her somehow? I don't know. I wouldn't worry too much about it though, stranger things have happened." Jamie said reassuringly. "Just consider it a blessing."

I still had so many questions, but for now, I decided to take Jamie's advice so I could enjoy my current state of excitement. I just couldn't believe that I somehow managed to land not one but two jobs in my first week here in Boston. I was beyond ecstatic.

Chapter 23

⚜

I called Jamie to share the news and she decided we should celebrate with a nice dinner, so she stopped on her way home to pick us up a bottle of white zinfandel and lobster rolls. She said they were a must for any new Bostonian. She was right, they were out of this world! When she got back to the apartment, Jamie loaded Working Girl into the DVD player for us to watch and baked us some walnut brownies for dessert. She mentioned that she and Dillon had settled on plans for a lunch date and a ghost tour on Saturday afternoon. When she asked me to come along, I told her I had every intention of staying home this weekend to do my laundry and read my new book. I knew she didn't want me to feel left out, but I could tell she was equally as excited to have some time alone with Dillon before he went back to New York.

When Monday morning rolled around, Jamie woke me up early so we could go to the gym for the self defense class she signed us up for. We both learned some pretty effective maneuvers that would help us gain time on an attacker.

The instructor taught us that our best defense was to get as far away from the attacker as possible. The goal was not to stay and fight them, but to disarm them enough to get away and call for help. She also taught us to always be fully aware of our surroundings, since most attackers typically target those who appear to be vulnerable. The maneuvers we would learn over the next few weeks, would effectively take any attacker by surprise, because we are going to be much stronger than we appear. I found the class to be very insightful and was very much looking forward to coming again, the following week.

~

After class, Jamie and I utilized the Jacuzzi and sauna. I could literally feel all of my tension melt away. I thoroughly enjoyed the relaxation part and promised Jamie I would come with her to the gym again, sometime before our next class. When we returned from the gym, Jamie got ready for school and I stayed home to take a nap before my first day at Silver Linings.

"Good Luck on your first day, You're totally gonna rock it!" Jamie said, as she grabbed her bag off the couch.

"Thanks, I'm a little nervous, but Maggie said she would train me. Fingers crossed! I hope you're right!"

Jamie crossed her fingers. "Don't worry, You got this, Babe!" She called out to me as she walked out the door.

By now, it was 9:30 AM and I still had a few hours left before I had to leave. Before she left, Jamie helped me pick out a long and flowing styled, ivy green dress with layered sleeves to wear. She said the color really complimented my skin tone and hair color. I chose the same black stiletto flats to go with it, since I don't like wearing heels. Jamie had beautiful clothes, but she and I were very different when it came to style. This dress, however, was perfect for me. Given the choice, I would always choose comfort over style, any day of the week! Since it was my first day, I knew I really needed to dress the part. I considered myself very fortunate to have Jamie and her closet to get me through until I could go shopping for myself.

I cooked myself some breakfast and brought it outside on the terrace to read my book. Apparently, Jamie had moved my new candle to the table outside, and I couldn't agree more with her placement. She also left a lighter on the table. *How thoughtful?* She must have known I might come out here this morning. I lit the candle to add some ambiance for my reading session and after a few minutes, the sweet aroma nearly had me in a trance.

I found myself daydreaming about my encounter with Jasper at the park and began thinking about the dream I had about him. Just thinking about him brought me such tranquility. I couldn't help but wonder how he could have this effect on me. It was more than an obsession, it had to be! Something must have taken place in the cosmos the day we met because it really wasn't like me to obsess like this over a person. A favorite song or book, maybe, but never an actual person.

By 11 AM, the sun began to bake down on the lounge chair, and the formation of the clouds gave wind that it might rain. If I was to get a nap before work, now would be the time. I promised Maggie I would get there early. I stood up and took my breakfast plate inside and loaded it inside the dishwasher. When I went into the bedroom to lay down to set my phone on the charger, I noticed there was a text message notification.

Unknown Caller

🍀 *Hope to see you soon* 🍀

Clovers were a symbol for good luck. How odd would it be for Maggie to send this to me on my first day, working for her? I found it very strange, then figured I may as well add her number into my phone so it wouldn't read "Unknown Caller" anymore.

Me

Thank You. I'll be there.

I set an alarm for 12:30 PM and got in bed. It didn't take very long before I was asleep.

I was in the passenger side of a truck of some kind, but my hands were bound. I could feel a gnawing sensation from deep within as I silently tried to pull my hands free from the restrains with no success.

My head was covered with some sort of cloth-like sack, but I could just barely make out a figure between the stitches of the fibers. I swear it was AJ, I could smell the Jack Daniels in his perspiration. We had just made a turn and the vehicle began to slow down. The driver turned off the ignition and got out on his side of the truck. Shit!

The stillness in the air screamed impending danger when suddenly the door swung open on my side of the truck. I could feel his sweaty hands grab a hold of me and I screamed.

120

"*Stop screaming, you filthy little whore!*" *There it was, the evil demon, dwelling inside the dark side of AJ. I could recognize that voice from anywhere.*

I knew I was moments away from something very dark and dangerous. Though I had no idea where we were, or what I could possibly do to break free, I had to think fast. I reached my head over to where I thought the steering wheel might be and used my chin to slam on the horn.... BEEP BEEP BEEP!

Beep Beep Beep Beep, My alarm was going off. I let my eyes flutter open. My body was drenched in sweat and I could feel my heart beating a mile a minute. It was just a dream, I told myself, over and over as I began to slow my breath in an attempt to bring my heart rate back to normal. It was working. *Thank God.*

I needed to pull myself together, so I went inside the kitchen and turned on the coffee maker, before heading to the bathroom to turn on the shower. I could hear the voice inside my head again. "*You bitch! How could you leave me?*" It was as if he was right there in my subconscious. Remembering how many times I had turned to music for therapy, I shook my head and quickly turned on the radio to shut the voice out. Thankfully, the voice eventually disappeared.

Chapter 24

⸙

When I arrived at Silver Linings, I was five minutes early. I typically fared well with first impressions when it came to punctuality. It had always been maintaining the habit that I had trouble with. I was determined to correct that now that I had a job I could honestly be proud of.

First day jitters were normal at any new job for me. Today, however, I felt strangely empowered, despite the awful nightmare I had earlier that day. For the first time ever, I actually tried to fight back in my dream.

I'm totally going to rock this! I told myself in silence, standing there at the front door as I rang the bell. I heard a buzz, but no one was opening the door, so I opened it myself. Maggie was seated behind the desk she mentioned would be mine. I could hear her talking on the phone with someone as she motioned for me to sit down in the chair next to her. I was happy to see that the air conditioning had been fixed, just like she promised. When the call ended, Maggie turned to greet me.

"Carla, I'm so glad you could make it!" She said warmly before standing up to fetch a file from the filing cabinet, from which she produced a stack of papers and a clipboard for me to fill it out.

"These are just some formalities. You'll find an application and a list of rules and regulations you'll need to sign off on. I've highlighted all the areas where you'll need to sign and initial. You can try to fill it out in your downtime, while you are here or you can bring it home with you, but I will need to have it completed by the start of your shift, tomorrow, please."

"Okay," I said, taking the clipboard from her hands. "I also brought the documents you asked for, but I'm afraid I don't have any blank checks with me." I said as I reached into my purse to pull out my wallet and handed her my drivers license and social security card.

"Perfect. Don't worry, there's a form inside your paperwork that you can just fill out with your banking information, and that will do just fine as well." She said, while placing my license and social security card onto the scanner. "In the meantime, let me show you the switchboard and how it all works."

The switchboard had twelve separate lines. There were three live-in counselors on property and each of them had their own separate line. I learned that Maggie was the intake counselor. The other lines were streamed in for security, each of the resident houses, the staff lounge, the kitchen and the other offices.

At first I wondered if I might get overwhelmed by everything. Maggie said if whoever I was trying to transfer the line to didn't pick up, it would ring back to me and all I needed to do was write down a message for that person. She explained that no one at Silver Linings had digital voicemail because it was their mission to make sure that every voice was heard right away by an actual person. Residents were only allowed to give our number out to pre-screened emergency contacts. Some of the residents were given special cell phones to use that were monitored for security purposes, as well.

Along with running the switchboard, I would also have to buzz people in for both of the houses from time to time, like Maggie did for me when I arrived. I would always know when they were coming because they would first have to go through the security gate who would call to alert me. The security camera screen above my head would allow me to see all of the entrances of the property at any time. She told me to dial her extension if I had any trouble with anything.

Maggie answered all of the calls as I listened in for the first hour. Afterwards, she let me hold the reins and watched over me for the next hour. The majority of the calls that came through were to be rerouted. If ever someone called in that didn't specifically ask to speak to someone directly, I was to take down their name and phone number and reason for the call before I made the transfer to Maggie.

An hour later, I was on my own and feeling more confident in the training Maggie provided. I glanced over my paperwork a few times when it was quiet, but by the time my shift was over, I knew I would be taking it home with me.

At the end of the day, Maggie said I did great and let me go early since I had come in earlier. She seemed pleased to be getting some of her own work done. All in all, my first day at Silver Linings went very well.

As promised, I called my mother on my way home to tell her how it all went. She was very happy for me. When I asked to talk to Abby, she told me that she was rarely home anymore. Mama told me that Abby had a new boyfriend named Chase, whom she'd met, who seemed very nice. She sounded happy for Abby, but I could detect that maybe my mother was feeling a little lonely, now that Abby was gone most of the time. It was hard to imagine my baby sister with a boyfriend. I couldn't believe she was growing up and I wasn't there to see it. I made Mama promise to have Abby call me when she could find time in her new busy life. We both laughed, and she agreed.

~

By the time I got back to the apartment, Jamie was already home and cooking us dinner. She was making one of my all time favorite 'Jamie dishes', Tuna Casserole. The aroma filled the air as I walked into the front door and I immediately felt my stomach growl.

"Smells delicious, Jamie." I said, as I took my shoes off by the front door.

"Hey you, how did it go, today?" She asked, as I watched her wipe her hands off on a kitchen towel.

I plopped myself down in one of the dining room chairs. "Better than I could have ever imagined. I was much calmer than I usually am on the first day at a new job." I said.

"Maybe this job really is a blessing for you." Jamie said, as she took a seat in the chair next to me and handed me a glass of white zinfandel. It was my second choice for wine, but also a good pairing for our tuna casserole dinner.

"I still have a mountain of paperwork to fill out tonight, but I really think this job is a great fit for me. Their mission really hits home and I can honestly say that I feel proud to have the opportunity to contribute to it, even if it is just answering the phones." I laughed.

"Hey, that's just as important as anything else. Besides, maybe there will be room for advancement in the future." She argued. It was unlike me to be pessimistic about anything, and I loved Jamie for recognizing and deflecting it. She truly was a great friend.

"Good point," I said. "Care to help me decipher all of these rules and regulations I have to sign off on?" I asked.

"Sure thing, we can do it after dinner if you want. I have some work to do tonight, but I can spare some time to help out."

By 9:30 PM, I was exhausted. Between the early morning self defense class, my first day and all that paperwork, I really wasn't surprised. One of the forms I signed off on was an agreement for a background check and random drug screenings. That was a first for me, but also nothing I had any reason to be concerned with. The good thing was, once I was able to get past all of the red tape, this job would officially be mine and I couldn't be happier!

~

Just as I was getting ready for bed, my phone rang. I guess my mother kept her promise because it was my sister, Abby.

"Hey Squirt! How've you been?" I asked.

"I'm good. Mom told me you're in Boston?" She asked, sounding surprised.

"Yes, I'm staying with Jamie. She has a beautiful two bedroom condo. It's so different, but I think I am really beginning to love it here. Everything I need is within walking distance. You ought to see it! Oh, and I already have two part time jobs!"

"You do? Wow, that's awesome! So what about AJ? Is he there with you too?" She asked.

"No, it's just me." I paused. " I think AJ and I needed to take a little break from each other." I didn't want to worry her, so I didn't give her much about why we needed a break. "So… Mom tells me you have a new boyfriend? That's exciting…"

"His name is Chase. He's taking me to Homecoming, I can't wait!" I could hear the smile in her voice the second she mentioned his name which told me she was really happy.

"Leila, Kallie, Mom and I are all going dress shopping this weekend!" Leila and Kallie were Abby's best friends. They'd all been inseparable since grade school.

"How nice!" I said. "Please make sure to take lots of pictures and send them to me!"

"You know I will! I gotta go, I have a project that's due tomorrow. I've had it for two weeks now and I haven't even started it yet! Please don't tell mom." Abby said as she lowered her voice.

"Don't worry, your secret is safe with me!" I laughed, remembering all too well, those late nights I had spent cramming for projects in high school. "Good luck with your project! Love you, Squirt!"

"Love you too, Big Sis! Congrats on the new jobs!" She said, as we ended our call.

It was nice to hear her voice. I couldn't believe my baby sister was growing up so fast. Hearing how happy she seemed to be made me feel warm inside, but also kinda sad that I couldn't be there to see it.

I drifted off to sleep, with my heart full of joy, picturing Abby in her dress with her handsome date. Knowing she was truly enjoying her high school experience brought me a great deal of comfort. I knew, that wasn't always the case for everyone. I was also happy to hear that Mama would finally get to have some quality time with Abby and her friends over the weekend.

Chapter 25

M
aggie

GOOD MORNING, SUNSHINE

Me

Good morning

Okay, I'd be lying if it didn't strike me as odd to receive a 'good morning' text from my new boss. Then again, this was the same person who also wished me good luck on my first day. If this was the only strange thing about Maggie I had to bear, it wasn't anything I couldn't handle as long as the conversation didn't get any weirder. I laughed it off and went into the kitchen to make my coffee. Jamie was already up and sitting on the terrace nursing her own cup. She appeared rather pensive, as if she had something on her mind.

"Hey. You okay?" I asked, as I took a seat next to her.

"Yeah, I'm fine. I just haven't heard back from Dillon yet. He left yesterday morning. I just thought I would have heard from him by now," She sighed. "I guess I'm just a little worried."

"Well, maybe he was just tired when he got home. It's still early, I'm sure you'll hear back from him this afternoon." I said, trying to comfort her. I didn't like seeing her upset.

"I mean, it's not like he's obligated to check in with me, right? We haven't had 'the talk' about being exclusive or anything. I do really like him though, I thought we were hitting it off pretty well." It was easy to see, she was feeling insecure about their relationship, as anyone might, this early on.

"The chemistry between you two was plain as day from what I saw. You guys seem to make a great couple, in my opinion."

Jamie's face began to soften. She was clearly reminiscing about their time together. "You're right, I should probably just give it some more time." She paused for a moment, "I'm going to go to the gym before school today. I'm sure I'll feel better once I do finally hear back from him. I just hope nothing bad happened."

"I'm sure he's fine. Now go burn off some of that tension, it'll do you some good." I said "I gotta get going now too, anyway. Hope you have a terrific Tuesday!" I said cheerfully.

Jamie laughed, "My Corny Carla is back!" It was a nickname she'd given me back when we were in high school. I was never a big fan of it, but if my being corny brought a smile to her face, I was happy.

The coffee shop was really hectic. Probably one of our busiest days I had seen yet. You'd think that we would have made more tips with more customers, but that wasn't the case at all. People were grumpier than ever. In fact, if we had enough space, I would say we could have used some more help behind the counter.

Brooke and I barely had any time to talk and Ben offered no help, like usual. He stayed in his office most of the day. I was thankful when I finally got my break. Since it was very hot outside, I decided to bring my breakfast over to one of the comfy chairs in the bookstore to read for a little while, rather than walking over to the park.

By the end of our shift, Brooke and I finally had a few minutes to chat while we waited for Ben to give us our tips from Friday. He was on the phone giving a new delivery driver for our supplier directions in what seemed to be his best Spanglish. It was clear that Ben was frustrated.

Finally, after rolling his eyes at us, Ben reached up on the shelf above his head and handed us each our envelopes. Brooke wasted no time at all in opening her envelope. As it turned out, we totally banked at $47 a piece. Score!

I told Brooke about my new job and she congratulated me again before she had to leave. She had plans to go dress shopping for her sister's upcoming wedding.

"That sounds exciting, when's the big day?" I asked.

"It's been changed several times already, but as of right now, not until March." She laughed.

"Well send me some pics, I wanna see what you decide on" I said, as we each said our goodbyes.

Chapter 26

⚜

I gasped when I arrived at my office at Silver Linings. Maggie looked confused. I could easily understand why she wouldn't make anything notable out of the vase full of Gardenias staring back at me on my desk. Of course, it was of no significance to her. To me, however, it was a very clear indication that it might be a clue into finding out who, as Jamie pinned, my 'secret admirer' could be.

"Are you alright, dear? You look as though you've seen a ghost" Maggie asked.

"Oh, yes. I just…. love gardenias." I said, laughing nervously. "They're so beautiful!" There was no way I was going to inform her of my real suspicions. It was made very clear that security was their highest priority at Silver Linings, and I wasn't sure if this so-called 'secret admirer' was even a threat. Not yet, at least..

"So do I. My nephew was here this morning. He mostly maintains the grounds, but don't be surprised if you find him doing other odd jobs from time to time. He's the one who fixed our air conditioning.

Jack of all trades, that he is! We're very fortunate to have him around. He's made a routine out of putting fresh flowers out around the office to help invigorate our space, for years now. We all enjoy them, I do hope you're not allergic!" She said, expressing her concern. "It's not a problem if you are, I can easily tell him to skip your desk if need be."

"Oh, no... I'm not allergic, I love flowers! Especially Gardenias, they're honestly my favorite." I said, smiling.

"Oh good." She said, appearing relieved. "He rarely puts gardenias out, so I was honestly a little surprised to see them myself, as they do tend to wither easily." She said, while straightening the vase on the desk. "I'll be in my office with the blue vervain he left for me on my desk. They're sitting right next to the mountain of files I need to get to." She laughed, turning toward the hallway that led to her office "Please call me if you need anything."

I didn't let on that I was aware of how fragile gardenias were, but it was partially why I loved them so much. These were just as fragrant as the ones I had in the apartment, too. Their essence kept me wondering all afternoon if Maggie's nephew may have had any sort of connection to who my 'secret admirer' was. *Maybe it was all just a funny coincidence.* It was dumb of me to think so deeply into it. And yet, here I was, obsessing, once again.

For a moment, I found myself fantasizing that Jasper was my secret admirer. I pinched the butterfly charm on the necklace I was wearing between my thumb and my fingers. Oddly enough, the butterfly sensation returned to the pit of my stomach as if I had beckoned them at the mere thought.

I think my heart really wanted it to be him. *How on earth could he have possibly known where to send the gifts to?* If he had followed me home that day, it would honestly be kinda creepy. I shook the thought off and returned my focus to work.

Chapter 27

Jamie ordered us a pizza for dinner which must have arrived just before I walked in the door. It smelled as if it had just came out of the oven. I couldn't help but notice how tired Jamie appeared. No one wants to hear how tired they look, so of course, I wouldn't tell her that, but I would try my best to nonchalantly see if she was alright.

"Hey Jamie. Did you finally hear back from Dillon?" I asked, curiously.

"No. I haven't. I'm really worried now, Carla. What if something terrible happened?"

"I honestly thought you would have heard from him by now. I understand why you're concerned, but until you do hear from him, I would try not to worry so much. I mean, you did say that you guys aren't exclusive yet, right? And for his sake, if he ever does decide to pop back into the picture, he better not be ghosting you."

That was the problem with dating these days, no one had time for proper goodbyes anymore, they simply avoided it at all costs by dropping off the face of the earth. Whether something really bad happened or not, Jamie had every right to feel concerned about her relationship with Dillon. I know he meant a lot to her, I just didn't want it to break her spirit. If anyone deserved to be happy, it was Jamie.

"I guess you're right. I shouldn't waste all my energy on a guy who may or may not be 'ghosting' me." She said, while proceeding to open the pizza box to choose the biggest slice she could find to put on her plate. "What about you? How was your day at the office?"

I figured now was the best time to tell her about my rendezvous at the park with Jasper and Lucas. It was my turn to distract her with something that might help take her mind off of the situation she was in with Dillon.

I spilled all the tea and gave her every juicy detail, including the Gardenias that were sitting on my desk, waiting for me that afternoon. She drank every bit of it up as though she were trapped somewhere in the desert and just discovered an oasis. Jamie was more than fascinated by my tale.

"You're kidding me! Why didn't you tell me? It all makes perfect sense! What if Jasper *is* your secret admirer?" Jamie asked.

"I thought about that too, just this afternoon." I said. "But don't you find it a bit creepy, if he followed me home to find out where I lived?"

"Maybe. A little." She laughed, "You should totally go back to the park tomorrow. Maybe that's his usual spot to walk his dog."

Apparently Jamie didn't find it creepy enough, if she was suggesting I try to find him again. I'll admit, whenever those butterflies hit me, I just might be bold enough to try and find him intentionally. Most of the time I was too chicken. After all, it did take me an entire week to open up to tell Jamie about him in the first place. It was no secret, I was the type of girl who was extremely shy when it came to the opposite sex. I guarded my heart behind a booby-trapped castle, with fiery dragons to boot! Even AJ had to chase me down in order to catch me. Admittedly, I thoroughly enjoyed a good chase, as I watch through stained glass windows to see if my suitor was brave enough to come find me.

"I don't know, Jamie. I do want to see him again, but I don't want it to seem as if I'm looking for him, ya know?" I said.

"Because that would give away to the fact that you might actually like him?" She asked as if she'd learned something brand new about her best friend of over twelve years. "I get it. So maybe you'll run into him again, sometime. I wish we had his last name so we could at least look him up on social media." Jamie said with a mischievous smile.

"Yeah, I ran before I really had a chance to get to know much more about him. I didn't know what else to do when he asked me about my bruises" I said.

"I can understand why. You were backed into a corner. It makes sense to me that you weren't ready to tell a complete stranger that you'd been abused by your former boyfriend. I guess if fate will have it, it will find a way." Jamie conceded.

"Yep, pretty much what I've been telling myself this whole time." I chuckled.

We both went to bed early that night. It felt good to let Jamie in on everything I had been holding on to. It wasn't that I was hiding it from her. It was more like I needed to process things in my head first. There was a distinct element of significance to my fantasy life when I held it close to my heart, though. Like a great work of art, I was possessive over it because I didn't want anyone to taint it in any sort of way. Without any outside influence, there was no way anyone else could come along screw it up for me.

~

The next day, I found another text message from Maggie. She must have sent it to me after I'd fallen asleep.

Maggie

DID YOU LIKE THE FLOWERS?

Yet another strange text message. I knew that we had clearly gone over this fact, just yesterday. Maggie was my boss now, though, so I had to reply back as if we hadn't already had the conversation about my love of gardenias. I just kept it short and simple.

Me

Gardenias have always been my favorite :)

The aroma of coffee drew me out of bed quickly. Jamie was already dressed and appeared to be in much better spirits than the day before.

"Dillon finally texted me back last night." She hummed, excitedly before I could even ask her what had her smiling so brightly this early in the morning.

"Oh… I presume everything is okay, then?" I asked, as I took a sip of my coffee. It was perfectly warm, with just the right amount of milk to soften the boldness of the taste and the perfect amount of Splenda to sweeten it up. It gave it that perfect caramel taste I love. I always found it funny, that whenever I got coffee anywhere else where it was made for me, it never tasted as good as if I had prepared it myself. I had concluded that it must be the perfect measurement. As I let that fact dawn on me, I vowed to be more precise at work to try to make my customers happier. Happy customers equaled better tips.

"He said he had accidentally left his phone at a meeting with one of his clients and couldn't get it back until last night" Jamie said. She seemed convinced of the excuse he'd given her. While I, on the other hand, had my suspicions all over the place. I certainly wouldn't tell her that though. She needed everything to be okay. So for now, until I had more clarity, I would keep my scattered thoughts to myself on this one.

"I'm so glad he's alright. And more importantly, that you are smiling again." I said.

"He also said he might be coming back in two weeks!" She sounded so excited. "I'm so glad I didn't call or text him more than like three times, or he might surely think I was a nut!" She laughed. "The silence definitely drove me crazy, though." she added.

"I'm very happy for you." I could only hope and pray for Jamie's sake that my suspicions were all lies formed by my own insecurities about love.

Chapter 28

T he week flew by. I wasn't sure if it was because I was working so much or that perhaps the moon was in one of those crazy phases where time just seemed to go by faster. Nonetheless, today was finally Friday, Payday! To say that I was excited was an understatement. Jamie and I had plans to go out for brunch and shopping on Saturday. I honestly couldn't wait for the weekend.

After work, Brooke and I went to lunch. This time it was my treat. She wanted pizza again, which was fine by me, despite having it for dinner the night before. I had plenty of tips saved up to keep me going, so I planned on keeping the money from my check in the bank.

While we were waiting for our pizza, I opened the envelope containing my paycheck. It was $132.56 after taxes which seemed decent enough, considering my first three days at the coffee shop, I had earned over a hundred dollars in tips.

It clearly wasn't enough to live on, but with the added income from my new job at Silver Linings, I could surely make it work. One thing I knew for sure, I was in far better financial shape, than I was when I I had first arrived. At least I would be soon. Whether I would stay here in Boston would all depend on what Jamie and I would agree upon, as far as rent.

Brooke passed her phone over the table to show me the dress she settled on for her sister's wedding. "I love the dress, but why does she want us all to wear this hideous mustard yellow? Like who picks yellow for their wedding colors?" Brooke cried out in a whiny tone. She had a valid point.

"Oh wow! That is pretty! I agree, though. Your sister could definitely have chosen a more suitable color for her bridesmaids. Not everyone can pull that color off." I agreed.

"Maybe she just wants us all to look ugly compared to her. She needs to get over her damn self!" Brooke continued her complaining.

"Well, I don't know your sister, but I wouldn't be surprised if, perhaps, she is feeling a little self conscious about how she looks. After all, this is the biggest day of her life. Maybe you can try boosting her confidence? Feed her compliments on how she looks in her dress before asking her to change the color of yours. I wouldn't wait too long, though. Alterations take time." I said, trying to offer my best advice.

"That's not a bad idea, actually. Thanks." Brooke said.

After lunch, Brooke and I shared the leftovers and said our goodbyes. I thought it would be nice to bring some pizza home for Jamie.

Chapter 29

Whken I arrived at the office, Maggie greeted me with a huge smile. "I'm so glad you're here," she said. "I just got word that you passed your background check. The job is now, officially yours. Congrats, kiddo!"

'Kiddo', it was a term of endearment my stepdad had also given me. For a moment, I could almost feel his presence beside me. I swear, that man was probably the most honorable guy I had ever come to know in my entire life. Our family was completely devastated when he passed.

I could still feel his spirit with me on many occasions. His influence on my life helped me realize I deserved so much more than what I had with AJ. I'd even go as far as saying that if I hadn't known Joel, I'd probably still be back in Virginia, allowing AJ to continue crushing my soul.

"Oh, wow… thank you!" I said happily.

I knew I would pass my background check, but knowing the red tape side of things was all over with had brought me a great deal of relief. I couldn't wait to tell Jamie the news when I got home.

"Welcome aboard, officially." She said smiling. "You'll come to know soon enough, that here at Silver Linings, we love to celebrate! Some of the residents are baking you a welcome cake, in the kitchen as we speak."

"They are?" I was surprised. It really made me feel special, and also a little silly if I might add.

"Yes, they sure are." She said, "I figured I would give you heads up, in case you don't like surprises. We will be having a small welcome party in the conference room for you, later. A reason for us all to eat cake," she laughed, " all kidding aside, though, we are all truly delighted to have you onboard with us, officially."

"That's very nice of them. Thank you." I said. *Seriously?! An office where the staff looks for any reason to eat cake? Sign me up!* It couldn't get much better than that. I didn't let on, but I was really looking forward to the cake too!

"Just do me a favor… Act surprised, will ya?" She winked. "Until then, I will be in my office. You know how to reach me!"

I was managing the calls that came through pretty well now and rarely had to call Maggie anymore, but it was nice to know that she was happy to help out, if need be. At 5:30 sharp, Maggie called me into the conference room to "help her set up for an *important meeting* in the morning" as she called it. I was well aware it was a ploy to get me in there without knowing what was really going on. I had no trouble at all in playing along. Her secret in revealing the surprise was safe with me. I grabbed the cordless phone to take with me, in case any calls came through and proceeded down the hallway to where Maggie had previously shown me where the conference room had been.

What I wasn't prepared for, however, were the deep blue eyes staring back at me when I opened the door to the conference room. *Jasper!* I swear, time stood still for a moment. I completely froze. Thankfully I was playing the role of being surprised, which just so happened to be a great disguise for everyone else in the room. At least for everyone but Jasper, who clearly knew there was far more behind my reaction than being surprised. I felt the magnetic pull in my core return to me in full force. And like magic, the butterflies have re-awakened.

"Welcome Aboard, Carla!" They all shouted.

Snap out of it, Carla! I quickly turned my gaze away from Jasper. There were a dozen other people in that room. I could look at anything or anyone else but those captivating blue eyes. Ahh, the cake! I found the cake and held my attention there, until I could maintain my composure.

The cake was iced in white and beautifully decorated with a beautiful assortment of flowers all around it. 'It's OFFICIAL!! Welcome to the team, Carla!' had been artfully written in red and blue on top. The cake looked so beautiful, as if it were made by a professional baker. I felt so warm inside from the kind gesture, but my emotions were running all over the place. All at once, I was happy, nervous but most of all, in complete and utter shock.

I kept my focus steadily on the cake, as my eyes lit up in awe. "It's so beautiful! Thank you all, so much." I honestly had to shake away the tears from forming in my eyes.

We all sat there at the large marble table with enough black leather chairs to seat twelve people. Jasper was one of the few people left, standing around as Maggie passed around slices of the cake. I tried my best to keep my eyes away from him, knowing fully well the intensity of the impact I felt inside by his mere presence alone. Undoubtedly, I would expose myself had I let my eyes wander into his again.

Nearly the entire staff was there, along with a few of the teenage residents, who I'd learned had each lent a hand in baking the cake. Everyone was there, except for Stuart, who was at the gatehouse holding down security. Apparently, he was promised the leftovers to bring home to his family.

Everyone seemed genuinely welcoming towards me. I got to meet the other two counselors, Angela and Michael, both of whom, I'd only spoken to a few times while transferring their calls to them. It was nice to finally put a face to their voices.

Then there was Gretta and Doris, who worked in the kitchen preparing meals for the residents. I had spoken to Gretta a few times on the phone as well. She was the one who handled the supply orders for the kitchen, while Doris was in charge of what was on the menu each week. Alexa, Jeremy and April took care of the general housekeeping and Caleb and Tony were both on the security team with Stuart.

They all gave me the feeling of a really close, tight knit family. Most of them were employed by Silver Linings for many years. I tried my best to say hello to each and every one of them with the exception of Jasper, who I kept my peripheral focus on for most of the party. I noticed he kept himself busy, talking with Caleb and Tony out of the corner of my eye. I could feel his gaze on me the entire time. It felt like I was basking in the glow of his sunlight. A sense of surrealness arose inside me like nothing I had ever felt before. An awareness I just couldn't put my finger on, it was almost as if I were high. It felt more significant than I ever had in my entire life.

The party was over by 6:30 PM. Maggie let me go home early since it was Friday. At some point, Jasper must have slipped out without me noticing because I didn't see him anywhere. Even though I avoided looking in his direction at the party, I kind of wished I had been able to catch where he may have trailed off to. I just wanted to see him, once more before the weekend.

Chapter 30

"You're never going to guess what happened to me today!" I beamed as I waltzed through the front door of Jamie's apartment as if it had somehow become enchanted with the magic I felt inside me.

Jamie was sitting on the couch, working on her laptop as usual. She already poured herself a glass of wine and quickly turned her gaze away from her computer. She let her eyes do her talking as she waited for me to continue.

I quickly poured my own glass of wine and sat down on the couch next to her. I proceeded to tell Jamie all about how my day went, including the guest appearance at the party. Astonished, she stared at me in amazement as she consumed every detail.

"Are you serious? Holy shit!" She blurted out. "Well, first of all Congrats on officially nailing the job! Which, let's be honest, we knew without a doubt you would pass that background check," she laughed. "But, Jasper?! That's the guy you met at the park with the dog, right? He was there, in the flesh, at your welcome party? You gotta tell me how that all went!" I could swear, Jamie was even more excited than I was, if that was even possible.

"I was in shock, I mean, it was kind of a disaster," I laughed to myself as I remembered the long pause I had given my audience when I first opened the door to the conference room. "I couldn't even look at him again because I was literally shaking! I introduced myself to everyone else but him." I said with a laugh.

Jamie laughed. "Aww! So you do have a serious crush on him, don't you?" Once again, Jamie was spot on! I could see it written all over her face, and felt myself begin to blush from embarrassment.

"No…" I tried to deny it, even though we both knew there was no getting out of this one. Jamie could read me like an open book with her eyes closed any day of the week and twice on Sundays.

"Okay, I admit, I may have had a dream about him, after we met. And I do get butterflies in my stomach whenever I do think about him, so if that means I have a crush, then so be it." I declared more to myself than Jamie.

"There's nothing wrong with having a crush on him, I mean it seems he likes you too! I'm willing to bet he's the one who's been sending you all of these gifts." She said.

Jamie's phone buzzed. She picked it up and began reading the text message she'd received aloud, announcing it like she was some reporter on the five o'clock news. "It's Breana. She's inviting us out to Club Hush tomorrow night. Alex is going to DJ and can get us all in for free again!" She turned her eyes away from her phone and looked directly into mine. I could see she was excited, but unsure because of how things went down the last time.

"Yes, let's go!" I said without hesitation. "I'm ready to celebrate!" I was also on a determined mission to make things right with Jamie's friends, even though they didn't know what really happened that night at the club. "I know exactly where my boundaries are this time, Jamie." I said, addressing the look of concern on her face. "All I have to do is refrain from going onto the dance floor. At least for now." I implored, well aware that Jamie wanted to protect me above everything else, even if it meant not going out with her friends when she really wanted to.

"Well, OK! But this time, we will take my car so we can leave whenever we want. I'm only going to have one drink so I can drive us home." She said, caving. She quickly sent a text to Breana, letting her know that we were in on the plans and that we would meet them there at the club.

"Sweet! Now we can also go dress shopping tomorrow after brunch." I said, realizing I didn't have all that much money to go shopping just yet. I had other essentials I needed to buy.

"There's actually a really cute boutique shop that sells gently used clothes. I have a member's club discount card too! It's where I got half of my clothes when I first came here to Boston and didn't have much money. It's not far at all from The Plaza Cafe, and brunch is on me tomorrow." Jamie offered. *Did she hear my inner thoughts?*

"That sounds perfect, but next time, brunch is on me!" I added. I didn't mind being treated every now and then, but only if I could return the favor. I was far too prideful to be a mooch.

"You got a deal." She said, turning back to her laptop. "Unfortunately, I have work to finish up tonight, otherwise I would watch a movie with you."

"It's totally fine, I was planning to finish reading my book and get some laundry done, anyway" I said. "I'll go find something to cook us for dinner." It was obvious that Jamie appreciated the way we complemented each other, just as I did.

That night, while folding my laundry, I heard a text notification come through on my phone. I picked it up to read a text from Maggie.

Maggie

WERE YOU SURPRISED TO SEE ME?

Wait a minute. There was no way that this was Maggie. It just couldn't be her, it doesn't make any sense. Come to think of it, nothing really made sense within these text messages I kept receiving from Maggie.

Me

I'm sorry, who is this?

Maggie

I THINK THE CAT IS OUT OF THE BAG NOW, DON'T YOU THINK? LOL

Holy shit! It's not Maggie, it's Jasper! So badly, I wanted to check all of the previous text messages to see if it all lined up. My mind was completely blown. I desperately needed some time to process everything before responding so I left the last text message to appear as if I hadn't read it yet.

Chapter 31

The next morning, Jamie brought me a cup of coffee. She placed it on my nightstand before taking a seat at the foot of my bed, making the mattress cave in enough for me to notice I wasn't the only one on it.

"Come on, sleepy head." She said in her best attempt to coax me awake. "It's 9:30 and we have places to go and people to see!"

I pulled the covers up over my head and turned over. "But it's Saturday...." I whined.

"I brought you a cup of coffee." She said, as she pointed to steamy cup on the nightstand. *Did she think I had x-ray vision to see through the blanket?* I could tell by her tone, though, she was getting pretty antsy.

If I knew Jamie, she was already up at the crack of dawn, been to the gym and back home by now. "Alright, alright. I'm up, I'm up!" I said, pulling the covers back down, revealing a very bright light of day. I took a few sips of my coffee and crept my way to the bathroom to shower. I got dressed and made my way out into the living room.

"Hey, do you think we can take my car this time? I have to drive it so the battery doesn't die." I learned that fun fact from Joel, when he taught me how to drive. "Plus I really need to get used to driving in the city. The roads are very different here." I asked, while retrieving my keys from off the hook that was hanging above the kitchen counter. A place for everything, and everything in its place. Living with Jamie was rubbing off on me. I found myself more organized than ever.

"Of course, we can. I'll just direct you where to go." Jamie replied as we each grabbed our purses and headed out the door.

The line at the Plaza Cafe was pretty long. The hostess said the wait was about an hour out, so we asked if they could give us a call when our table was ready. She agreed and handed us a buzzer that would notify us. The boutique store Jamie mentioned was only a block away. We decided to walk over since the weather was nice and we had time to wait for our table to be ready.

The options of clothing to choose from seemed endless. I knew I wouldn't have enough time to try them all on, so I let Jamie help me decide. My favorite choice was a gorgeous emerald green dress with a beautiful iridescent shimmer layer on top. It was a little more provocative than my typical style, but the moment I saw it, I knew I had to at least try it on. I could see it still had its original tag on it which meant that whoever donated it must have never even worn it. What a shame, because this dress was in a class all its own. I was impressed to have found it here, collecting dust at a second hand store.

Jamie's jaw nearly dropped to the floor the moment I stepped out of the dressing room. "Girl! You look like a mermaid!" She added a whistle at the end, the kind any pretty girl would hear while passing by a construction site.

"Seriously?" I asked while staring at my reflection. I stepped onto the platform with the three sided mirror, the kind that lets you see yourself from every angle. I slowly spun around to see the back. "Oh, I don't know, Jamie…" I said, brushing my fingers up the side of the split that came clear up to my hips. The cut in the back was just above my waist, and my hair fell perfectly in line with the seam. The dress had spaghetti straps, and the length went halfway up my thigh. The material on the inside was buttery soft and hugged my body true to form. The way the light hit the shimmer was what really gave the dress that wow factor. I thought I was out of my mind to even consider it. I caught sight of my new butterfly charm necklace in my reflection and was happy to see it paired well with the style of the dress. For a moment, I stood there recapturing everything had been revealed last night with Jasper's text message. Ironically, the butterfly sensation returned.

"Hell yeah, you look hot! This dress is perfect for the club tonight and with your gorgeous figure, you can totally pull it off! " Jamie said. "I'm buying it for you for your birthday!" She had that famous Jamie gleam in her eyes that dared me to even think about challenging her decision.

"Oh my God, I totally forgot my birthday was this week!" It wasn't like me to ever forget my own birthday, but with everything I had going on recently, I guess I could understand how it slipped my mind.

Still, I wasn't fully convinced on whether I could actually bring myself to wear the dress to the club that night, but I also knew that if Jamie said it looked good, she was probably right. Jamie was a straight shooter, one of those friends you knew you could trust to be honest. I was the same way. I always told the truth, because if it were me who was asking, I always wanted the truth. Jamie knew that.

We found the perfect silver sandals. The heel was low enough for my taste in comfort, and the shiny mirror design on them complemented the shimmer of the dress. Jamie added them to her shopping basket along with the dress, which meant she was buying for me too. Jamie found herself another winner with the dress she found for herself. It was a sleeveless, aquamarine colored dress that was sure to turn the head of any straight laced guy.

By the time we left the boutique, I scored two pairs of jeans for work at the coffee shop, three new dresses for work at the office, a couple pairs of slacks, three blouses and two pairs of ballet flats all for under $60, after applying Jamie's twenty percent discount. I can see why Jamie raved about this store, apparently, she was a pro at thrifting! I was completely hooked and planned on signing up for the discount club, myself, when the buzzer went off, telling us that our table was ready. By that time, we were both starving. We quickly finished paying and raced out the door to get back to the Plaza Cafe to ensure our table wouldn't be given away to the next people in line.

At brunch, I told Jamie about the text messages from Jasper. She was just as flabbergasted as I was. This whole time, the answer was right under our nose. She pinned it as fate, but we both felt it was almost too good to be true.

"This calls for a celebration! How about we go get our nails done?" Jamie suggested.

Since she already paid for my brunch, dress and sandals for the club that night, I could afford to splurge a little. I reasoned for a minute then decided to call it a birthday gift from myself.

It was nearly 3 o'clock when we finally made it back to the apartment. I was pooped. It felt like ages since I was able to buy myself new clothes. I felt so proud to hang them up in the closet. I had a ways to go, but this was definitely a decent start for my new wardrobe.

We decided a nap before dinner would be beneficial to refresh ourselves before our night out at the club. I was really looking forward to seeing Breana and Ryan again. Maybe this time, I would actually stay long enough to meet Mandy, Alex's girlfriend, whom I assumed would be coming too.

Chapter 32

J amie and I arrived at the club at 8:30, dressed to slay. Heads were turning left and right from both men and women. Breana called to let us know they were already there, waiting for us to come meet them at the rear entrance of the club, where we all entered the last time. I kinda felt bad for everyone who was stuck in line, not to say I didn't thoroughly enjoy the privilege of skipping it.

"Wow, you girls look hot!" Breana said, as she guided us to the lounge area, where Ryan, Alex and Mandy were seated on the couch. Someone must have taken the liberty of ordering our drinks, because they were sitting on the table waiting for us when we arrived.

"Back atcha, Babe!" Jamie shot back. "Ow Ow Ow!" I swear Jamie must have been a guy in her past life, she was never short of cat calls.

Breana was wearing a candy apple, red cocktail dress and black stiletto heels that had to be at least four inches high. If we were hot, she was most definitely scorching.

"So glad you girls could make it, this is my girl, Mandy." Alex said, as he stood up to formally introduce us.

"Hi" Mandy said, stretching out her hand to shake each of ours.

"So glad we could finally meet," Jamie said, taking the lead. "I'm Jamie, and this is my best friend, Carla."

"Hey Mandy, nice to meet you." I said, offering a smile as I shook her hand.

Mandy had shoulder length, dark brown hair and she pulled it back into two braids one on each side of her face. Her eyes were green and her adorably freckled face and fair complexion had me believing she was fresh out of high school. I was sure she had to at least be twenty-one in order to be allowed inside the club. She wore a pale pink spaghetti strap tank top that bared her midriff with a pair of baggy jeans and a black and silver studded belt. She finished her look off with a pair of black combat boots. I could easily see how Alex was attracted to her. The two of them paired nicely in their grunge style.

"Well, I'd better get going, hope you all enjoy the show!" Alex called out to us before heading off to set up his stage area.

I felt very different than I did the last time I was here. My feet weren't hurting nearly as much and with all I had to celebrate, I really did come to party.

"I see you remembered, thank you!" I said to Ryan as I reached over to grab my sea-breeze from off the table. I was impressed by Ryan's ability to remember what we all drank the last time we were here. I guess it naturally comes along with being in the service industry as I, too, remembered everyone's drink order.

"You betcha!" Ryan winked.

"I'm the designated driver tonight, so I'm only going to have one or two, this time." Jamie said, as she took a sip of her rum and coke. We all found ourselves a spot on the sofa to sit down. We could hear Alex testing out his equipment on stage when the club began to dim the lights.

"So what have you girls been up to?" Breana asked.

"Same old, same old. Work and school, at least for me, anyway." Jamie replied. "Now Carla, on the other hand, has been quite busy establishing herself, here in Boston. She's already landed herself two jobs and a hottie who seems to be rather taken by her." She said, wasting no time at all to blast me out to everyone.

"Really?! All that in two weeks? That's impressive! Congratulations!" Breana said, with a raise of her eyebrows.

"That is pretty impressive." Mandy agreed, smiling. "Congrats, Carla!"

"Thanks," I said, while attempting to straighten my dress, I was still feeling a little self conscious. "But uh...Let's not forget your own recent developments," I said in retaliation. I never felt comfortable having all the attention on myself. I had to throw Jamie into the spotlight.

"Oh yeah?" Breana asked, sounding intrigued. "Please, do tell!"

"Oh yeah! Did you by chance happen to see the guy I was dancing with, the last time we were here?" Jamie asked.

"You mean the gorgeous guy in the yellow shirt? How could we miss him, he seemed really into you when you guys were dancing." Breana asked.

"Yep, that's him. His name is Dillon. He's a real estate agent. He and I exchanged numbers and went on a few dates. We really seem to be hitting it off." Jamie said smiling.

"Well it sounds to me like you both are getting quite the attention." Breana teased. "So will Dillon be joining us tonight?"

"No, he lives in New York, actually, but he told me comes here often for business and to see his friend, who lives here."

"Oh, wow…. And how do you feel about the long distance thing?" Breana asked.

"It's actually not that bad. He's supposed to be coming back in a couple of weeks." Jamie replied, grinning from ear to ear.

"Aww, I'm happy for you, Jamie." Breana said. "Next time he comes down, you should invite him to come out with us so we can all get to meet him."

"That's a great idea! I'll definitely ask him when I talk to him tomorrow." Jamie replied.

Once Alex started the music, everyone began to pour inside the club.

I nearly finished my drink and thought about heading up to the bar when a cocktail waitress appeared asking us if we needed anything.

"Yes, I think another round is in order. By the way, drinks are on me tonight! Shots anyone?" Ryan asked us all, as he handed the waitress his credit card.

"Yes! Let's do shots! How about some Lemon Drops?" Breana asked the group, excitedly.

"What's a lemon drop?" I asked, curiously.

"It's basically vodka and lemon juice with a sugar rim. You'll love it!" She replied.

"Okay, sounds good to me." I said and everyone else agreed.

When our shots arrived, Jamie made a toast to my birthday, once again, shining the spotlight on me.

They all sang the Happy Birthday song and for the first time ever, I downed a whole shot all at once. It was harsh, but the sweet sugar rim made it tasty. Afterwards, Jamie asked everyone to come over to our place on Tuesday for game night and birthday cake and everyone agreed.

Not long after all the birthday shenanigans, everyone decided to head out onto the dance floor. That is, everyone but Jamie and me. I may have been tipsy, but I still kept to my boundaries. I certainly didn't want a repeat of the last time we came here.

"You should get on out there too!" I said. "I'll sit here and keep an eye out on our drinks. I don't want you to miss out on all the fun, just because I'm here."

"Are you sure?" Jamie asked, reluctantly.

"Yes, yes! Go have fun!" I reassured her.

"Alright, if you insist!" Jamie conceded as she scooted herself off the couch to go find the others.

~

Alex crafted such a chill vibe with the songs that he was playing. Between the drinks and the music, I was feeling alright. Right up until I noticed a familiar face sitting at the bar, across the way. From where I was sitting, I was able to catch a side view, but I was ninety nine percent certain it was Jasper. I would notice his face anywhere. You would think I might be happy to see him there, and at first glance, I truly was. Until I noticed who was sitting next to him. I'd never seen her before, but she was beautiful. She had long pin straight blonde hair with fair skin. She was dressed to kill, in a form fitted black cocktail dress with slits on each side to reveal her rib cage, and cherry, red high heels.

Judging by her body language, she was clearly into Jasper. Her legs were crossed inward towards his body and she kept on doing that hair flip thing while she was talking. Jasper's body language was more straight, however. It almost seemed like he was uncomfortable with her bodily advances. Not enough to convince me, however, that her behavior wasn't reciprocated. I wasn't sure if it was the liquor inside me or straight up jealousy, but I could feel my blood begin to boil at what I saw.

Feeling restless, I ordered another drink when the waitress came around then I downed it as soon as she brought it to me. I couldn't take much more of watching some gorgeous bimbo of a girl flirt with the guy I've been obsessed with over the past three weeks. With liquid courage coursing through me, I ventured out onto the previously, self prohibited dance floor in hopes to find Jamie and the rest of the gang.

Chapter 33

T he dance floor was packed tight, like a can of sardines. It was a challenge to even attempt to move through the crowd. In a bit of frustration, it occurred to me that perhaps instead, I might be able to steal Jasper's attention away from 'blonde bimbo' by dancing on the outskirts of the dance floor.

I was never one to put myself out there, I honestly wasn't much of a dancer. DJ got us falling' in love by Usher was playing. One of my favorite songs. *How appropriate? Thank you, Alex!* I slowly let my body catch the rhythm and closed my eyes. I put my hands up in the air while swaying my hips back and forth. This wasn't so bad, it kinda reminded me of how it feels when you first step into the pool and the water slowly begins to warm up. In keeping my eyes closed, I felt a little less self conscious about my amateur dance moves. As I slowly began to open my eyes, I was surprised to see that my plan had actually worked. Jasper was staring right at me from across the room. His icy blue gaze was intense, as if he bore a hole straight through me. I felt the churning inside my belly as I dared not change a thing that I was doing. As long as I had his attention on me, I was more than good.

I couldn't help but laugh when I noticed the 'blonde bimbo' shift her attention to the guy on her other side, now. The minute Jasper locked eyes with me, he stood up and began to head in my direction. As he made his way over to me, it felt like the two of us were the only ones inside the club. Everyone else suddenly became a faded blur. He was only a few feet away when I felt the hands of someone grab my hips and begin dancing behind me, yanking my attention away from Jasper. I turned away from his intoxicating gaze to find Eddie, the guy who had sent me running the last time I was here.

I swear, this guy must really have it out for me, and yet there was just something about him that really turned me off. Still, knowing he was a friend of Dillon's, I didn't want to be rude so I turned to dance with him for a moment. I was instantly put off by the stench of his Jack Daniels laced breath. I turned to face Jasper when he rested his hand on my shoulder, stealing me away from Eddie.

"Hey you!" He said, pulling me in towards him.

"Hi" I said, grinning like some goofy teenage girl with backstage passes to her favorite boy band concert.

Eddie, attempting to claim me for himself, pulled me back in a quick and sudden move. Instinctively, my body resisted his moves. I could feel the tension in the air rising as Eddie clearly didn't take kindly to the interruption of our dance. *Great!* The last thing I needed right now was for these two to brawl on the dance floor and ruin yet another perfectly good evening for Jamie and her friends. I shot Jasper a look that implored that he not entertain Eddie's advances at picking a fight. It was evident, by the clenching of the muscles in Jasper's jaw, how difficult it was for him to back down. Still, he managed to keep his composure and thankfully conceded to my unspoken request.

"Let's get out of here." He said, taking me by the hand, whisking me off the dance floor. He didn't wait for me to respond and I was perfectly okay with that.

~

We both made our way out through a side exit of the club. By this time, it was pouring down rain just like the day we met. Jasper tucked me under his arm to shield me from the rain as he guided me towards the canopy that covered the valet station. I watched as Jasper reached inside his pocket to hand the valet guy his ticket and a twenty dollar bill, before asking for his keys. Relieved of the task of getting soaked, the valet serviceman was more than happy to oblige. It was plain to see he was also thankful for the generous tip he'd received for simply handing over Jasper's keys.

"Wait here for me." Jasper said as he ran out into the rain.

After a few minutes and what seemed like an eternity, I noticed a white Mercedes SUV pull up into the valet station. Between the dark tint of the vehicle and the copious amount of rainfall, it was difficult for me to see who was driving the vehicle. When Jasper jumped out of the driver's side to come around and open the passenger side door for me, I was shocked.

Had I known it was him, I would have never let him get out in the first place. He was already soaking wet from the rain. I don't know why, I just never imagined him to have an expensive luxury car. He seemed so… down to earth.

"You know, you didn't have to do that. I'm sorry, I just didn't know it was you." I said, as I pulled the seat belt across my chest and over my lap.

"Don't apologize. Here, put this on before you catch a cold." Jasper said, as he retrieved a dark gray hoodie from the back seat of his SUV.

I caught a glimpse of his ripped chest and well sculpted six-pack abs when he removed his sopping wet, white button down shirt. Shortly after, he produced another matching hoodie to the one he gave me and pulled it up over his head. I was quick to turn away when he caught me staring.

"You get a good show?" He asked, playfully.

"You must hold stock in gray sweatshirts, huh?" I said, hoping my joke might take the attention off my face which had already turned red hot from embarrassment. I quickly pulled the hoodie up over my head to cover it up. His sweater felt so soft, warm and luxuriously comfy as I wrapped it around my cold wet shoulders. Now I understood why he had more than one. Even better that it smelled as if it were actually him who was deliciously draped around my body, like a blanket on a cold and snowy winter night.

"Nah, I just like to be prepared for stormy weather and hot chicks that are soaking wet." He laughed, proud of his clever response.

"Touche!" I said, as I silently let my mind wander into the gutter.

I could feel the magic in every fiber of my being. An electric force bounced between us like a ping pong ball in the confines of Jasper's SUV. It reminded me of a firefly that had been trapped inside a glass jar. I wanted to savor every second. I wouldn't dare let him know, but I was trying my best to capture this very moment for my 'never forget' memories. I had been writing them all down in a locked journal ever since I was eight years old.

Jasper turned on some music and we drove off into the dark and stormy night. I could almost hear my mother's voice, screaming at me inside the back of my head, warning me not to get into a car with a stranger, but I quickly shut the voice down. I had no doubt, I felt safe with Jasper. I wasn't sure why, but this feeling was very distinct. I felt it the first day we met and I could also feel it now. It just felt like I was... *Home.*

Chapter 34

⚜

The fact that Jamie would surely be looking for me by now had temporarily escaped me. I was quickly reminded, the moment we pulled into the parking garage of our apartment. *Was Jasper driving me home?* I was confused, but I didn't say a word.

After pulling into a parking space, Jasper turned off the ignition and set his gaze upon me. Bringing with it, a sense of longing, a thousand horses could not hold back. A pulling sensation from deep within my core flew to me in an instant, as the butterflies were all running rampant now.

"There's something that..." Jasper paused and looked up as if he were trying to thoughtfully consider what he might say "uh, there's something I've been wanting to do, since the first time I laid eyes on you." His voice reduced to a low growl as he leaned in toward me. *Holy Shit!*

"Oh yeah?" I asked, turning inward to allow him full access. "What's that?" I felt my heart beat pounding inside my chest. I could feel my hands were slightly shaking, when he tugged at my chin and pulled me in for a kiss, so sweet, so tender, as our lips greeted hello for the very first time. It was no indicator, however, of the kiss that followed. Burning hot with desire as our tongues united in a journey to explore every inch of each other. I was the first to break, as my breath hitched inside his. *Breathe, Carla, breathe!* For a moment I thought I was dreaming. *Had I died and gone to heaven? In fact, there they were, the pearly white gates just over... no that's his teeth. Get a grip, Carla! This is not your daydream fantasies, this is real!*

"You're trembling," he said, taking my hand in his as he rubbed the pad of his thumb over my palm. "Let's get you upstairs so you can change into something warm and dry."

"Okay. Just one second." I agreed, letting myself drift back down to earth as I pulled my phone out of my purse. *Yikes!* There were three missed calls from Jamie. "I need to text my best friend and let her know that I'm alright. Is that's alright?" I asked.

"Of course. You don't have to ask." Jasper replied, while he gathered all of his wet clothing into a plastic bag he retrieved from the center console.

Me

Hey Jamie, I'm back at the apartment. I can't talk right now. I'll fill you in on everything tomorrow.

Jamie

Thank God! I've been looking all over for you. I'm glad you're alright, but you definitely have some explaining to do in the morning.

Me

Of course, you're never gonna believe this one! I'll talk to you in the morning. Have fun, tell everyone I'll see them next time for me, please!

Jasper came around to open the passenger side of his SUV while I was still texting Jamie. Chivalry, an experience I truly believed only existed in the books I read, or the movies I watched, was something I now had to get used to.

I desperately wanted to learn what knowledge Jasper had on me, so I continued to follow his lead. When he typed in a pin number for the elevator, I was in utter disbelief. When he pushed the button for the twelfth floor, I could no longer keep my mouth shut.

"Hold on... Wait a minute, Do you actually live here?" I asked.

"Yes, I do. It's not a problem, is it?" He asked. *Oh. My. God. Had he really lived here, in this building, the entire time?* Jamie was literally going to freak out. I don't know how I did it, but somehow I managed to conceal the fact that my brain was headed straight into overdrive. *Keep your cool, Carla!* I told myself as I stood next to him in the elevator, silently putting together all the pieces of what had been puzzling me for nearly three weeks.

"Nope, not at all. It's just that... Well, this is where I live too." I said.

"Yes, I know," he laughed. "Are you okay with coming upstairs with me for a late night snack? I promise to behave. I make a killer grilled cheese sandwich and tomato soup, " he said, smirking. Somehow, I got the feeling it was more than food he wanted to snack on, but he wasn't alone on that!

"That actually sounds amazing." I replied. *Pssh.* As if he even needed to tempt me with food, I thought, laughing to myself. That was just an added bonus.

The elevator dinged and opened straight up into his apartment. *Seriously, did Jasper really live in the penthouse?* I couldn't help but wonder how he could afford such a nice place, working at Silver Linings. I didn't want to be rude, so I figured I would wait to ask him about it for now.

Jasper's apartment was enormous compared to Jamie's. The floors were of swirly gray and white marble and everything appeared to be quite pristine and modern looking. It had an open studio floor plan with a spiral staircase that led up to his master suite. His kitchen was twice the size of Jamie's and had an Island in the center with four bar stools on the outer side.

You could have a full on conversation with someone cooking in the kitchen while seated comfortably, on his soft, white leather sofa in the living room. In front of the sofa, stood a chic, white marble coffee table, large enough to fit a 1000 piece puzzle and still have room for a centerpiece. There were a few books and magazines on top, but nothing else. I couldn't help but stare in amazement. It must have cost him a fortune to furnish this apartment. Everything appeared so elegant and clean.

"Do you live here all by yourself?" I asked curiously. And as if I had beckoned him, Lucas quickly came running up to tower over me.

"Lucas! Down!" Jasper called out as he physically had to tear Lucas off of me. "Well, as you might remember, I do have a roommate. A very rude one, might I add." Lucas was licking me like crazy and I was hysterical. "Apparently he's excited to see you again. Though, I'm not surprised. I would be too." Jasper said, laughing.

"So it's just the two of you then?" I asked, demanding clarification.

"Just the two of us. The bathroom is off to the left. There are some towels in the drawer if you'd like to shower while I make us something to eat. Just wait here a minute while I get you something dry to wear." He said, dragging Lucas up the spiral staircase, leaving me with the perfect opportunity to quickly look for any clues I could find that might tell me a little more about who this man was I had been obsessing about for weeks.

Sitting atop a fully stocked bookshelf, an old Polaroid photograph of a very young Jasper caught my attention. It was taken of him when he was a little boy, maybe six or seven years old. He was nestled inside the branches of an old oak tree with a wide grin of sweet satisfaction, written all over his face. My guess was that he was proud of the climb he had just made. That smile could melt the heart of any warm blooded woman, young or old. The photo reminded me of the old oak tree back home in Virginia. I found that rather peculiar.

A moment later, Jasper came back down the stairs holding a pair of gray sweat pants and you guessed it, another matching gray sweatshirt. I just laughed and took them from his hands. "I'm not saying a word!" I snickered and went off to the bathroom that Jasper had pointed out to me earlier.

The shower had a slate gray interior with black cobblestone flooring and white grout. It was equipped with one of those rain down faucet types. I was surprised to find the water pressure was actually perfect, in spite of the faucet. I let the warm water wash over me as I recounted the past hour we'd spent together. As high as I had climbed to the top of cloud nine, I didn't want to keep him waiting too long for me, so I stepped out of the shower in search of a towel in the drawer. It felt so luxurious, draped around my naked skin. So soft, I couldn't help myself from reading the tag to find it was made of Egyptian cotton.

Everything about this bathroom screamed luxury. After wringing my new dress out in the sink, I carefully hung it to dry on the hook of the back of the door and pulled on the sweatshirt and sweatpants that were each two sizes too big for me. I wrapped my hair up inside the towel around my head and made my way out of the bathroom.

I found Jasper seated at the Island. As promised, a large bowl of steamy tomato soup and a perfectly crafted grilled cheese were sitting there, waiting for me. I wondered how long I had been in the bathroom, as his own sandwich and soup had both been left untouched.

Jasper stood up to pull out a stool for me. "Would you like a glass of wine?" He asked while he retrieved two of the wine glasses that had been hanging on a rack above the Island.

"Yes, that'd be lovely." I replied as I nonchalantly adjusted my rear onto the stool. He poured us each a glass of Chianti and came back over to the side where I was sitting.

"You know, there *are* drawstrings on those pants," He said as he slowly reached over to tug at the strings, pulling them tighter around my waist. I swear, I would completely melt like putty in his hands if he had wanted to go any further. He was a perfect gentleman, though and I could only respect him more for that.

I took a bite of my grilled cheese to spare myself from having to speak. *Mmm.* He wasn't lying. I was no stranger to a good grilled cheese sandwich, but this one most definitely gets the blue ribbon of all time. Instead of eating his own, he just sat there and watched me with that burning gaze of his. The color of his eyes were dark now, almost violet.

Through and through, this man was the epitome of gorgeousness, but those eyes are what really had me in trance. "Delicious! Aren't you going to eat?" I said, feeling alarmingly flustered at being the center point of his attention.

"Yep, sure am!" He said, taking a bite of his sandwich as if he could sense my feeling overwhelmed. Even the way he ate, had me reeling. It was carnal, like a wolf with prey. The air between us gave way that we were both completely enraptured by each other's company. I needed to do something to lighten the mood, because the way things were going, it wouldn't be long before he carried me up to his bed. I knew I wanted to have this feeling again, and soon. I felt strongly, however, about not giving it up on the first date. No, this wasn't a one night stand type of deal. I wanted far more than that and if I wasn't mistaken, he did too.

I took a sip of wine and scanned my brain for something we might be able to talk about, without getting too heated.

"So how long have you lived here?" I asked.

"Almost four years. What about you? I haven't seen you around for very long, I definitely would have noticed." He replied, far from shy about declaring his observation.

"I actually just moved here a few weeks ago. I'm from Virginia." I answered.

"I had a feeling you weren't from around here. You still have that cute southern twang in your voice. So what brings you here to Boston?" He asked, appearing genuinely intrigued.

Shit. Should I tell him? Probably not the best first date material. Wait, was this even a date? "My best friend, Jamie, goes to college here. I'm staying in her apartment on the 7th floor." It was the truth, just not all of it.

"Oh yeah? and how about you, no college?" He asked.

"Well, my step dad passed away unexpectedly, back when I was in high school, so I had to help my mom out a bit with my college fund." I replied.

"Oh wow, I'm sorry to hear that." He said consolingly. "And your mom? Is she here in Boston, too?" He asked.

"No, she lives with my baby sister Abby. Well, I suppose she's not a baby anymore, she's sixteen. They live in Virginia." I laughed. "What about you, do you have any brothers or sisters?"

Small talk was working. I could feel my body temperature begin to cool and settle from the burning hot coals it had been,, just moments before.

"No, I was an only child. My father died when I was two. He was out to sea when a storm came in unexpectedly and overturned his boat. Unfortunately they never recovered his body and my mother... well, she didn't take it very easily." He paused, searching for my reaction, "she eventually died of a drug overdose when I was five. Aunt Maggie was my legal guardian, for most of my childhood. I grew up on the Silver Linings Property."

I quickly fought a tear threatening its release, as I could only empathize about everything he had just revealed to me. Here I was making small talk, where he was literally pouring out his heart and soul to me. I felt so ashamed for not wanting to open up about AJ. It wasn't that I didn't feel I could trust Jasper, I just wasn't ready to unpack the emotional trauma AJ had left me with. I certainly didn't want to burden him with it, either.

"Jasper, I'm so sorry. I can't even begin to imagine what that must have been like, growing up without your parents."

"It's alright." He said. "It was difficult as a child, but I've had extensive therapy, one of the perks of living at Silver Linings, I suppose. I'm in a good place about things now, though. It took me some time to learn... Sometimes, bad things happen to good people and we have no control over them, but we can always grow from them." They were words that seemed far wiser than his years. I was staring directly into the face of the work that Silver Linings provided. They healed Jasper from his childhood trauma.

My spirit was beginning to warm up to the knowledge that I may have landed myself the job of my dreams. The question was: *how did my placement in the position relate to Jasper?* I just had to know.

"I guess you're right. Still, it must have been hard to come to terms with everything, especially at such a young age, I'm sure."

"It wasn't always easy... God bless Aunt Maggie. I definitely gave her a run for her money in the beginning. Unfortunately, I didn't fully come to terms with everything until after I made some poor choices as a teenager which led me to more extensive counseling." Jasper said, admittedly with a sigh.

"Oh, I'm sure. But you had a lot to get over, so don't be too hard on yourself about it. I'm sure she understands." I said, pausing for a moment to imagine what sort of trouble Jasper could have gotten into as a teenager.

"Forgive me if I'm being blunt, but I have been wondering... Did you follow me home the day we met at the park?" I asked, shocked by the courage that came to me to ask *that* question. Relieved, however, that it was finally out in the open, I eagerly awaited his response. My question sparked interest in Jasper's expression as he raised his eyebrows at me.

"Well, I'm not a creep. If that's what you're asking." He laughed. "You made it clear you didn't want to be followed. After you ran off, I waited for the rain to settle down to head back home, myself. On my way back, I noticed you left your folder out on the bench, where Lucas stole your hot dog. I grabbed it in case I was ever able to return it to you. When I got home, curiosity got the best of me. I found your resume and thought you'd be perfect for the open position at Silver Linings, so I retyped it and submitted it along with a short, but glowing recommendation letter. I knew that was all Maggie needed to consider you a good candidate." My jaw dropped. *My resume!* Of course, it had all the information he needed for everything. My phone number, address, everything. It all made perfect sense now. *How on earth, after nearly three weeks, can the mention of one word 'resume' be the missing link to piece it all together?*

"The rest was all your own doing. Please don't be upset with me and tell Maggie, though. She'll kill me if she finds out that it was me who sent it in and not you." He added. I could tell he wasn't very fond of being vulnerable, just like me. I quickly put his mind at ease by kissing him on the cheek. *Chicken!* I should have gone for his lips.

"So you're not mad, then?" He asked, working up a smile.

"Mad? You literally made my dreams come true! With my experience, I never could have landed that job, had you not done that for me." I wasn't mad at Jasper one bit, in fact if anything, it was quite the opposite. I was extremely grateful to him.

"Thank God. It's been weighing on me all week! I'm so glad you're not angry with me." He said, sounding relieved.

After we finished eating, I was getting tired. It was quite a bit of information for me to process all at once, but I was feeling content about everything. Now that I knew Jasper conveniently lived upstairs, I knew for certain I would see him again, at some point. I figured it best to go back down to Jamie's apartment for the night.

"Wait, let me walk you down. I've gotta take the monster out anyway." Jasper offered. He dropped me off on the seventh floor and kissed me so hard, I felt dizzy. I nearly fell out of the elevator, butterflies in tow.

"You have my number, text me tomorrow morning when you get up!"

He said, as the elevator doors were closing.

"I will." I called out as I made my way over to Jamie's apartment.

Chapter 35

It was just past midnight when I walked through the door. Jamie was still in her dress, so I imagined she must have just gotten home from the club.

"Oh good! You're here! Come out on the balcony with me really quick!" I said. "Hurry!"

"What's going on?" She asked, as she hopped off the couch to follow me out onto the terrace. Her voice, carried off with the breeze that picked up as we both stepped outside.

"Shh… He might hear you! Look! Down there." I whispered, pointing down to the sidewalk.

It was dark outside, but the street lamp illuminated the sidewalk just enough for Jamie to get a good glance at Jasper and Lucas walking down the street.

"What are we looking at? The guy down there, walking his dog?" Jamie whispered.

"Yes! That's him! That's Jasper!" I said, trying to keep my own voice down.

"Shut up! That's him? I know that guy.… Well, I don't exactly know him, but I've seen him around before. He lives right here in this building."

"I know, I literally just found out tonight, when he took me home from the club. Come back inside, I don't want him to hear us talking about him."

"You're so silly. We're seven stories up! There's no way he can hear us from all the way up here" She teased, following me back into the living room. I filled her in on nearly every detail of how my night went with Jasper. The look of shock that spread across her face proved she was just as dumbfounded as me.

"Honestly, I was kinda mad at you for leaving the club without saying anything. I was so worried you had another breakdown. Now that I know how everything went down, I can't even blame you. Especially the situation with Eddie. I'm definitely going to have a talk with Dillon about it, " She said.

"I know, I'm so sorry for leaving like that. I just didn't know what else to do. I didn't want to see them fight. That was the last thing I needed, especially since I ruined things the last time we all went out." I let out a sob, as the tears pooled inside my eyes. I was happy how my night turned out, but still felt frustrated about having to ditch out on Jamie's friends again.

"No, honey. You didn't ruin a thing!" Jamie said as she reached over to put her arm around my shoulder. "It wasn't your fault, you had a lot on your plate. Your wounds were still fresh from AJ. Please don't beat yourself up about it."

"So what did you wind up telling everyone?" I asked, as I wiped the tears out of my eyes. I hated crying in front of people, even Jamie.

"Don't worry, they were out on the dance floor having a great time when I noticed you were gone. I just told them you'd gotten a ride home and that you wanted me to tell everyone goodbye before I left." She answered.

Consoling enough, Jamie's words did bring me some relief. I really wanted to leave a good impression on Jamie's friends so that I could one day call them my own.

"Okay." I said. "Well, it's been one hell of a night, I think I'm ready to go to bed." To be honest, I couldn't wait to be alone with my thoughts.

"Well, that makes two of us." She agreed. "Good night."

I was too emotionally exhausted to write, but it was important to me to get it all out on paper, while it was still fresh on my mind. I pulled my journal out of my duffle bag and set it out on the nightstand, hoping it would remind me to write everything down the following morning.

Every intimate detail Jasper and I shared resurfaced in my mind, as I drew the inner side of my elbow over my eyes to smell the sleeve of his sweatshirt. Enchanting myself in his essence, I let myself drift away.

With his scent, I could easily recall the intimacy we shared inside his SUV, and the way he kissed me so sweet and tenderly that first time. I could still feel the electricity coursing through my veins that was present, the moment we unleashed our passion for one another on that second kiss.The mere thought made my spirit dance like no one else was watching.

The way Jasper expressed his care for me, not only by his words, but also his actions, spoke volumes to me. I caught myself comparing it to the relationship I had with AJ. Granted, this was the first time Jasper and I had spent any time together, romantically. It clearly demonstrated that what I wanted and deserved out of love was not only out there, but in the realm of possibility. Only time would tell what might become of us, but one thing I knew for certain... I would never again, go back to what I had before coming here to Boston. Not with AJ, not with anyone, ever again.

Chapter 36

❦

U pon waking, Sunday morning, I wrote everything down in my journal. Savoring every morsel of detail like a girl who was about to go on a diet that had just been given her last piece of cake. I devoured it! By the time I finished writing, I had easily filled eight and half pages in my journal. A record for anyone else, mentioned before in this journal.

Writing had always been an indulgence for me, and when it came to writing my own personal recollections, it was even more special to me, because it was like reliving it all over again.

This journal was filled with many of my sweetest memories. In my world, to be mentioned in it, was quite the honor. Being the only one to ever lay eyes on it, I kept it under lock and key.

Today, the words danced across the paper, faster than I could write them. It was like my fingers were magically possessed by a deep seeded purpose of portraying Jasper as my knight in shining armor. If my journal had been the palace of my life and I was the queen, Jasper was most certainly my king.

I reached across the bed to grab my phone off the nightstand as I remembered him asking me to text him when I woke up. I couldn't believe it was almost noon. I figured by now, he would surely be awake.

Me

Good Morning.

Jasper

Good morning, Beautiful. Did you sleep well?

Me

Actually, yes. I did, thanks! How about you?

Jasper

Aside from a little snoring from the beast, aka Lucas, I did too. I couldn't stop thinking about our last kiss in the elevator. I had half a mind to come back upstairs and make you change your mind about spending the night. Lol

I was happy to see he had finally grown out of the all caps theme he'd been in. I read his text message three times over before I could muster up a reply. I swear, this man must have a written contract with the butterflies in my stomach. I had goosebumps all over, just reading his text!

Me

That's funny, because that same kiss you couldn't stop thinking about nearly did the trick! ;)

Jasper

Do you have any plans for this evening? I have a few projects I need to wrap up over here at the office, but after that I would love to have you over for dinner, if you'd like.

Me

Are you really working on a Sunday? I asked, trying to make him sweat it out.

Jasper

I wouldn't be if I had you to entertain me this morning ;) So will you come over for dinner? Please?

Me

OK, but only if you let me bring dessert

Jasper

Done. Dress comfortably and bring your appetite. I'll see you tonight at 7.

Me:

OK, I'll see you then.... P.S. Try not to work too hard

After showering, I got dressed and came out into the living room to find Jamie curled up on the couch, watching television. Since I had arrived in Boston, we rarely did anything more than relax and watch movies on Sundays. It was the only day that Jamie took solely for herself, after juggling work and school all week.

"Good morning, sleepy head. I made us some scrambled eggs and biscuits" Jamie said.

"Good morning." I replied making my way into the kitchen, hoping that fresh coffee was still a part of this breakfast equation. "I hope you don't mind, but I won't be here for dinner tonight." I called out from the kitchen. The coffee pot was still warm, so I still had my hopes, until I tasted that it was a little on the burnt side. *Could be worse, ahh... it'll just have to do!*

"Hmm, let me guess, you have a hot date?" She asked, teasingly.

With my coffee cup in hand and a giant smile on my face, I sat down on the sofa next to Jamie. "As a matter of fact, I do." It should be noted, I was also blushing. "Jasper invited me over for dinner tonight." Jamie gasped.

"He did? Like upstairs, in his apartment?" She was giving me that 'someone's gonna get lucky tonight' stare.

"Yes, he did. I'm excited... I'm also terrified!" I admitted, laughing nervously. "I told him I would only come if I could bring dessert."

"Oh you'll bring dessert, alright and I'm willing to bet he won't be able to get enough of it!" She had that devilish grin that instantly recaptured the heat in my cheeks from just moments before. "All kidding aside, what are you planning to bring with you?"

"At first, I thought of Dillon's delicious Nutella Strawberry Shortcake, because it was so yummy, but now I'm leaning more towards chocolate cake because who doesn't love chocolate cake, right? Besides, what if he's allergic to strawberries?" I asked, inhaling sharply through my nose, fighting the wave of panic that attempted to emerge.

Sensing my anxiety, Jamie put her hand over mine. "Hey, don't overthink it. Go with the chocolate cake, it's going to be so scrumptious he won't want to eat any other chocolate cake again... Just be sure you save some batter to bake me some cupcakes. I'll need to liven up my night here alone with my DVD player." she winked. I got the feeling there were more ways than one to decipher Jamie's cryptic words. "Besides, I'm pretty sure we have everything you'll need right here, up in the cabinet." She added. Then again, maybe it was just me who sought more meaning out of what she was saying. I silently laughed at myself. It was Jasper's words that had me all fired up this morning, not Jamie's. *Get a grip, Carla!*

"OK, chocolate cake it is, then! Thanks Jamie." I said, jumping up to return to the kitchen to make my breakfast plate. All this talk about cake was making me hungry.

After breakfast, I got to baking the cake so there would be enough time for it to cool down enough for me to ice it. Jamie and I spent the rest of the afternoon watching movies. I also did my laundry so I could return Jasper's sweats to him at dinner. I didn't really want to give them back, but I didn't want to be rude and just assume he'd let me keep them.

When 6 o'clock rolled around, I was relieved to remember Jasper telling me to dress comfortably. I took a moment to wonder if he somehow knew I would stress about it. At least I wouldn't drive myself crazy trying to find something I thought he might like to see me in.

Dressing comfortably was easy for me. I paired black leggings with a white cami tank top and my soft, lavender sweater, in case it got chilly in Jasper's apartment.

I sent a quick text message to Jasper letting him know that I would be making my way upstairs shortly.

Me

I'll see you in a little bit

Me

P.S. I hope you like chocolate cake!

Jasper

Who doesn't? 😋 *Come up when you're ready. I'll be waiting ;)*

I brushed on some nude eye-shadow and light mascara and swiped a bit of shimmer frosted lip gloss on my lips. My hair naturally had that beach-wave look that most girls would kill for, so I didn't even mess with it. One look in the mirror and I knew I had nailed the 'girl next door' vibe I was going for. Not that I had much doubt, this was the style I mostly lived in, anyway. For good measure, I figured I would ask Jamie's opinion for the added boost of confidence, I knew I could count on her to deliver.

"Do I look alright?" I asked, as I twirled around in the middle of the living room floor.

"You look gorgeous, as always!" she said polishing my ego. "Oh, by the way, I have a beautiful crystal cake platter, with a matching cover, up in the closet. You're more than welcome to use it if you'd like. Just be careful with it, it was my great grandmother's." She said, pointing to the pantry. "Oh my God! You have got to try one of these cupcakes! They're out of this world!" She cried, with her mouth full of cake. As much as I wanted to dive into one myself, to make sure it was perfect, my nerves were high up on a cliff, anticipating my date with Jasper that was just a few short minutes away.

"I'm afraid I'll have to take your word for it. I have to get going, I don't want to keep him waiting." I called out as I searched the pantry for the platter Jamie mentioned I could borrow. I found it way up on the top shelf and carefully brought it down to the counter in the kitchen. Knowing it was a family heirloom, I was extra cautious when I relocated the cake. I really wanted it to present well, and the platter really did the trick! "The cake looks beautiful on your Grandma's platter, thanks so much for letting me use it!" I said, gratefully.

"Of course! Now go get your man hooked on your gorgeous cake!" She said, winking at me. "Just do me a favor, please. Text me if you plan on staying the night so I won't freak out in the morning, if you're not here. Oh, and you have to invite him over for your birthday on

Tuesday!" She added. The idea of even asking him to come had me on edge, since it was only our first date. I knew Jamie would never let me live it down if I didn't at least ask, so I agreed.

"I haven't even told him about my birthday yet, but I'll see what he says. And no, I'm not planning on staying the night." I laughed. "I do have my key though, so you don't have to wait up." I added, as I carefully made my way through the front door with the cake in one hand and Jasper's sweats in the other.

Chapter 37

I typed in the pin code Jasper gave me and hit the button for the twelfth floor. The desire to see Jasper, brewing inside me all morning, had managed to effectively shove my anxiety onto the back burner, where it evaporated into a scant vapor. I couldn't believe that in just a few minutes, every fantasy my mind had created about this guy would soon become my reality.

Those oceanic blue eyes of his propelled me deep into an infatuation the moment they first caught my attention. So intense, that his presence somehow found its way into the realm of my dream world. It's no secret that the eyes are a window into the soul, and in his, I could easily dive to the ocean floor in one foul swoop.

Something spectacular happened to me the day we met, I could feel it deep within my bones. It was as if the magic of life had miraculously returned to my body. I felt more alive than I had ever felt in my entire life. And now that his identity had finally been exposed, as my secret admirer, my anticipation only grew wilder, morphing into an unwavering obligation to discover where it all might lead.

The elevator dinged and opened up into Jasper's apartment. I could tell by the mouthwatering aroma of garlic and fresh basil, that Jasper had chosen to cook us dinner rather than order out. I took a moment to appreciate that Lucas was upstairs. Had he jumped up on me, like he did the last time, I probably would have dropped the cake and Jamie's Grandma's crystal platter would've shattered to a thousand pieces.

"Hey you!" Jasper said, turning his attention away from a pot he had simmering on the stove. The white tank top he wore flauntingly, showcased his perfectly sculpted upper torso and competed with the light washed blue jeans that left just enough for my imagination to run wild.

I couldn't tell which made my mouth water more, the aroma of the food or the glorious view of the chef. Intoxicated by my desire, I needed to sober myself up before I imploded. Keeping my cool, I carefully placed the cake and Jasper's sweats on top of the kitchen island counter and tried my best to ignore the magic, enveloping every pore of my skin. I took a seat on a stool to steady myself.

"Hey... I brought the cake with me." I said, doing a fair job of masking my current state of foolishness.

He walked over to my side of the island and gave me a quick peck on the cheek. "It looks delicious. As do you. Would you care for a glass of wine?" *Umm... yes, please!*

"That sounds nice." I replied. My nerves had now rejoined my desire for Jasper. It was hard not to notice, as they united in a perfect storm in the sea of mixed emotions inside me.

"I hope you like Italian." He said, as he wiped his hands off on a kitchen towel. He poured us each a glass of wine and placed mine in front of me. I took a sip and watched as he turned back toward the stove. At least *he* had a creative distraction. I started to wonder if he could feel the magic too.

"Whatever you're cooking smells fantastic! Can I help you with anything?" I asked.

"Nah, it's almost done. Just relax and drink your wine. It's almost ready. I hope you brought your appetite with you." He said. *Boy, did I ever?* In more ways than one, I most certainly did. I wasn't sure what had come over me, but in my current state of mind, I was hungrier than ever. *Get a hold of yourself, Carla! Drink. Your. Wine.*

"As a matter of fact, I did." I said, smiling. "I hope you aren't fond of girls who barely touch their food, because one thing I'm not afraid of, is eating." He turned around to raise an eyebrow at me.

"Then you're in the right hands, because I didn't bring you here to watch me eat." He wasn't laughing, he was serious. The heat of his gaze, effectively unraveled everything I did to try to keep my cool.

"I… uh, I brought your sweats back." I gulped, gesturing to the folded pile on top of the island. "They're clean, I washed them."

"You could have kept them… As we've already established, I hold stock and have plenty more." He said playfully. Detecting my unease, he turned off the stove and slowly stalked over to me like a tiger with prey. Coming here was dangerous. Delightfully dangerous, I'll admit.

He slid in behind me as he whispered in my ear. "You look beautiful, by the way." His words were simple. It was the way he had spoken them, that sent shivers through my ears and all the way down my spine. He took a sip of his wine and slowly placed it on the counter, while pulling out a stool to sit down next to me. Not a single movement was lost on me.

"So tell me, how do you like it here in Boston, so far?" The balance and control he was capable of, to maintain a normal conversation, while I was ready to completely lose it led me to wonder just how many more women he'd charmed before. I could swear, this man was as seductive as a playboy model to a prisoner who'd been locked up for life, without parole.

"Boston..." I took another gulp of wine, "Boston is nice." *Boston is nice?! Seriously?* "No, I mean it's good." I was digging my own grave. I could hardly even think straight anymore. "I mean, I really like it here. So far... that is."

"Why don't we finish our wine on the couch. Maybe you'll be more... comfortable?" He suggested. While I was fairly certain that was a *bad idea,* my head was so far into Lustville to even try to protest.

"Okay, yeah." I choked out as I stood up, wine in hand following his lead onto the gorgeous white leather sofa that stood in the center of the living room. I looked around. "Where is Lucas?"

"He's upstairs in his crate. I didn't want him knocking you over when you got here."

"I see." I said, still grasping for something, anything to say to rescue myself from my current state of being. By that time, I was convinced my brain had completely abandoned ship, and my body was utterly at Jasper's mercy.

"You seem nervous," he said, as he curled his left hand around my shoulder and brought his right hand up to my face to cup my chin, in a silent plea to put his lips on mine. His hands felt like sorcery, strong and slightly calloused against my soft skin. When I didn't protest his advance, he went in at full force. I closed my eyes. Somehow, everything I had been afraid of turned out to be exactly what I had needed. And he knew it! *Oh, boy did he ever know?* I could feel my body begin to soften as he gently caressed my face while we kissed. The desire between us, hot like molten lava, flowing down a volcano, into a fiery river, until he broke away and pulled back. When I opened my eyes, he gazed into them as if he were reading my soul. "There, now do you feel better?" He asked.

"Yes," I said, as if it were more than just a statement. "Yes, thank you. Much better." *Hello brain, so nice of you to rejoin us!*

"Good, because as much as I would love to throw Lucas out of my room and take you upstairs, right this very moment, I don't want our food to get cold." He laughed. I was in for it, for sure! I thought.

"Yes, I'm starving." I said with a laugh.

"Me too, let's eat, shall we?" He said, as he stood up to make his way back over to the kitchen to get our plates. I gathered our glasses of wine and brought them over to the end of the white marble, eight seater table that stood in the center of the dining room, just left of the kitchen. There was a vase filled with a beautiful arrangement of

Gardenias on top, just like the ones he'd sent me. Jasper set our end of the table up, with our dinner plates and silverware settings and sat in the chair next to mine.

"By the way, those are for you. I'm sure the ones you had are gone by now." Jasper said, motioning to the flowers.

"I was wondering… How did you know that Gardenias were my favorite?" I asked, as I twisted my fork around in a bed of fettuccine. It was evident that he'd made the sauce from scratch as it was packed with so much flavor. I could swear the tomatoes, veggies and basil smelled so fresh, as if they were freshly picked from a garden. Deeply impressed, my mouth was watering before I could even bring the fork to my mouth.

"I didn't, I'm just reminded of that angelic face of yours whenever I see them." I found it funny that he compared my face to angels, because that was exactly how I saw him, too.

"This sauce is amazing! Where did you learn how to cook?" I asked forking another bite into my mouth, this time adding a bite of meatball into the mix. "Mmm…" A moan escaped me. Every bite was like edible foreplay, I just couldn't contain my reaction.

"Well, I told you that I grew up on the Silver Linings property. We grow a lot of our fruits and vegetables on the property to help save on grocery costs. I had lots of time when I was a kid, so I learned all that I could from the people who worked there. My childhood may not have been traditional, given my situation, but I did try to make the most of it." Jasper replied. "I'm happy you like it."

"Like it? I love it! In fact, it's even better than my own and I love to cook too!" I said.

"Do you, now?" Jasper raised an eyebrow at me as if he were challenged to a dual. He was so damn sexy and he knew it. He wasn't at all arrogant about it, though, which only made him even more irresistible. If there was one thing I couldn't stand ,more than lying, it was arrogance. I couldn't help but notice just how different Jasper was than AJ. *Carla, stop comparing!* I quickly redirected my thoughts to respond.

"Yes, in fact I do. I started cooking and baking when I was around nine. Mama use to let me cook our family dinners from time to time. I always saw cooking as a form of art though, so I never follow recipes to a tee. I used to get a kick out of seeing my family's reaction to my dishes. Obviously, there were a few bombs along the way, for sure!" I laughed, taking notice how Jasper's eyes began to twinkle, as he hung on to every word I spoke. He seemed fascinated by what I had to say. A sudden wave of heat flushed over my body as I felt him watching me.

"Well, maybe next time you can come over and cook for me. Or better yet, maybe we can collaborate and prepare something together." He suggested. I'll admit, the idea of being within close proximity of both Jasper and food in the kitchen sounded so exhilarating to me.

"I would actually love that!" I said, taking note of just how compatible we seemed to be with one another, so far. It felt so natural, aside from the magnetic attraction bouncing back and forth between us. I wasn't at all used to being seen or heard, as if what I had to say mattered more than anything else in the moment. My relationship with AJ had been so different. We would always fight and argue, and half the time, I felt invisible. I was intrigued and wanted to know so much more about

Jasper.

"So... forgive me if I'm being invasive. Of course you don't have to answer," I paused, trying to gauge his reaction as his expression challenged me to continue. "I guess I was wondering how you are able to afford all of this if you work at Silver Linings?" I was embarrassed the second the words escaped me. I could feel my face turning beet red, it wasn't at all like me to be so forward. Jasper only looked amused by my discomfort.

I was never one who was concerned about money, like many other girls. I believed that the journey of life was in how I grew from each struggle I endured. Working and contributing my part to the household gave me a strong sense of purpose. Although, towards the end of my relationship with AJ, it felt like everything I had earned was necessary just to keep us afloat, especially with his daily drinking habits. That part never bothered me much, though. I felt it was my duty and hoped that AJ would have done the same in return, if it was me who was out of work. Not that I required a budget for drinking.

"You don't have to apologize, it's a fair question. My father was a fisherman. He wasn't loaded, by any means, but one thing he did have was a hefty life insurance policy. It was left to my mother and when she died, everything was left to me. I wasn't made aware of it until I turned twenty-one, when I gained full access. I technically don't need to work at all. I'm just not the type to sit around, wasting my life away. I like to keep busy, which is why I do a lot of volunteer work. Mostly at Silver Linings, because I feel I owe my life to them, but I do other charities as well from time to time. I also have a few investments that help keep my income regenerating."

His response pretty much explained everything I had been wondering about. Typically, I was a good detector of bullshit, and what he revealed was anything but that. It seemed pretty clear to me that Jasper was being honest.

Chapter 38

I insisted on helping Jasper clean up. We were both so full from dinner. Jasper suggested I find us a movie to watch on Netflix so we could let our food digest a little before diving into the cake I brought. Afterwards, he went upstairs to let Lucas out of his crate. He came charging down the stairs so fast and jumped right up on me to plant me with kisses. "Lucas!!! I swear, this dog!" Jasper shouted, as he too made his way down the stairs. I could only laugh. Every stroke of Lucas's tongue made me tickle.

Once the dust finally settled, we both made ourselves comfortable on the couch. Having Lucas there with us had really helped my nerves settle. I could finally relax!

"I had trouble deciding on a movie. Which one would you choose? The Karate Kid, The Goonies or Stand By Me?" I asked. They were all popular classics, hopefully he'd bite on at least one of them.

"Interesting choices" He laughed. "I actually loved all three of them. Let's go with The Goonies" *Thank God he's more decisive than me!* I thought to myself, as Jasper started the movie.

After a few minutes of watching, Jasper reached across my lap to grab the pillow that was behind me and stretched out to lay down on his side. I could feel my temperature rising as his strong forearm caressed my bare shoulder. "Come here," He said, pulling me in to be the little spoon. I loved the way he directed my body, to keep my nerves from going haywire. It made it so much easier for me to submit to his request.

The warmth of his body wrapped around me felt so surreal. *Like, was this really even happening right now?* I could honestly die, happily in his arms. The way he held me made me feel so safe and secure, it was like…. Home? I purposely selected movies I had already seen a thousand times over, because my focus was nowhere else but on him and how it felt to be near him. My body was so relaxed, I literally fell asleep.

When the movie was over, Jasper gently stirred me awake by the light strokes he splayed across my arm. I turned over to see his face, and there they were, those heavy lidded sapphire eyes that spoke an entire language of their own. He was hungry for a taste of my lips as he drew upon them with his rugged finger tips. "God, you really are beautiful" He said, pressing his lips into mine. A jolt of electricity shot through me, awakening the butterflies. They flew about, deep in my core, as if they had just been released into a forest in full bloom. Jasper stroked his fingers through my hair, gently twirling the strands around his fingers as if he'd discovered the texture of silk for the very first time.

Pressing his body into me, deepening the kiss between us, I could feel my body yearn for him like a five year old waiting to open her gifts on Christmas morning. He let his fingers glide down from my hair and onto my belly where he softly brushed his fingertips over my navel. He stopped to circle around a few times until he slowly made his way up to cup my left breast. He paused for a moment to gaze into my eyes, silently seeking my permission to go further. With eyes like his, any wish he'd made was easily my command.

My voice said nothing. Instead, I let my mouth do all the talking as we continued the dance of our tongues. Undoubtedly, I was his for the taking when suddenly, we heard a loud roar of snoring coming from Lucas who was sprawled out on the floor, snoozing away. We both laughed.

"Why don't we take this upstairs, while the monster sleeps?" He asked in a whisper, as he placed his pointer finger over his mouth. Far from denying him of any request, I carefully stood up from the couch, trying my best not to wake Lucas. Jasper followed close behind me, lightly pressing into the small of my back as he quietly guided me up the spiral staircase.

Chapter 39

❦

As night had fallen, it was nearly pitch black in the loft upstairs. I allowed my eyes to adjust to the dark. From what I could see, there was a smaller living space with a white leather love-seat couch and a matching recliner chair that must have completed the set from the wrap-around couch downstairs. An entertainment center equipped with a flat screen television and several gaming consoles stood against the back of the wall, next to the window that welcomed the light of the full moon.

Lucas's crate was positioned near the left side of the entertainment center and housed a large black and red plaided dog bed inside. The gaming controller on top of the small table that stood between the love-seat and the recliner chair gave me a clear indication that Jasper had probably spent more of his time up here, than he did downstairs.

With Jasper still behind me, I was guided through the doorway of a large master bathroom suite, with a two-way entry from the living room into the bedroom. A censored night light turned on when we stepped inside, illuminating a beautiful double sink vanity, made of dark gray and white marble. The vanity held several drawers for toiletry storage and had a large mirror on one side. On the other side, a gorgeous stand alone garden style bathtub was surrounded by step up platform trim. The trim of the tub was made of the same matching marble to the floor. Behind the tub, there was a window that had been draped with light, sheer, gray curtains.

The shower stall displayed an assortment of slated gray pebble stones and housed a sit down bench. A porcelain toilet with a privacy wall on each side separated the shower stall and the tub. I imagined that this was the bathroom of any real estate agent's dreams, the kind that was meant to sell the place.

Jasper closed the door behind us when we entered into the darkness of his master suite bedroom. Standing there alone with him, the slightest glow of the moon's pale light splashed across his face. I could feel my skin begin to prickle when he gently pushed me into a seated position on his four post Mahogany, California king-sized bed. The soft white feather down comforter pillowed underneath me as he stood there searching my eyes with his own. He lightly brushed the side of my cheekbone with his slightly calloused fingertips and carefully scooped a loose curl of my hair away from my face. His touch ignited a longing for his embrace I could no longer contain. Looking deep into his eyes, the only thing I could bring myself to say, was his name. "Jasper."

Bending slightly over me, Jasper aligned his face with my own letting his lips press into mine as he gently nudged me back into a laying down position on the bed. He slowly climbed on top of me, placing one of his knees between my legs and his other beside my hip, while planting feathery soft kisses from the side of my right ear, down to the swell of my collar bone.

I melted under his touch like a block of ice that had fallen to the sidewalk on a hot summer's day. His hands felt like magic on my skin as he brushed his fingertips underneath the thin spaghetti straps of each side of my cami and casually pulled them both off to the side. He caressed my shoulders from one side all the way to the other, following each stroke with kisses from his mouth.

The way Jasper touched me, made me feel so different than I felt with AJ, even on our better days. It was as if I could feel his emotions attached to each and every move he made. I could only surrender, letting a soft moan escape me. Undoubtedly, I had reached the point of no return. I let my hands softly tousle inside the waves of his hair, as if it held a cure for every aching need, I never knew I ever had. He slid my cami-top up over my head to expose my lavender silk bra. awakening goosebumps to form all over my body. Jasper brushed his fingers over the fibers of the silk. He cupped his hands over the fabric on each side of my breasts as he deepened the kiss to my mouth.

Suddenly a flash of light cast in through the window, followed by a loud clap of roaring thunder. In the light, I caught a full view of the beautifully chiseled jawline of his face and the sexy smirk he wore, as the sky conspired to conjure up its own storm to meet the one of passion in between us. In an instant, I was fully aware that the rain had the same effect on him, as it had on me.

"Are you okay with this?" He asked in a low throaty whisper, as he slowly reached behind my back to undo the clasp of my bra. Enraptured by the intensity, I was completely in tune with every want and need Jasper held for me, I could only nod in response.

Jasper slowly tugged the straps away from my shoulders, before pulling my bra down to reveal my naked breasts. Like an artist, analyzing his craft to find his next move, his beautiful eyes cast upon me. He nuzzled his face into the crook of my neck.

"You're so beautiful. My angel." He breathed in the faintest whisper to my ear, as he tantalizingly traced his finger tips around my bosom, allowing his palms to embrace my hardened nipples.

Slowly beginning to crumble beneath his touch, I reached down to the bottom of his shirt, pulling it only halfway up his athletically sculpted abs. It was as if we were playing a relay race when he met me in the middle to finish the task of pulling it up over his head. Enchanted by his beauty, I closed my eyes to burn this moment into my memory. Jasper bared down on me, kissing my mouth fervently, as though he needed my mouth on his as much as he needed the air in his lungs to breathe.

His hands swiftly fell to my waist, rimming the elastic of my waistband, while keeping his eyes pitched deep into mine, ensuring that I was okay with his unspoken suggestion. He carefully stood at the edge of the bed, pulling my leggings down below my knees and off over my feet. I was utterly at his mercy as he continued on to plant feathery soft kisses on me, from the center of my chest all the way down to my navel.

He lightly caressed the outside of my thighs and hips, letting his skillful hands make their way up beneath the sides of my panties. He stopped to let his eyes roam over my entire body, then back up, into my eyes.

Overcome with emotion, I let my head fall back onto the pillow as he began kissing his way down towards the lacy black trim of my lavender silk panties. He paused to nuzzle his nose along the flesh of my lower abdomen before slowly pulling my panties down with his teeth.

Jasper loomed over my entire naked body as if he'd just been given a backstage passes to my island of pleasure. The flicker of hunger inside his eyes magically unleashed every nerve I had in me, to scatter like ashes when he tucked my panties under the pillow, beneath my head.

The only thing that mattered in this moment was his attention to me as I craved his mouth on the most sensitive part of my body with every ounce of my being. The butterflies, lying in wait to worship his gorgeous lips, as they planted a short soft kiss to my clitoris.

He slid his tongue along my lips, parting me in sweet pleasure while letting his tongue meet in the middle with the pad of his thumb. Rhythmically pressing down onto my clitoris as he swirled his tongue around in a manner that had me shamelessly crying out in ecstasy.

Jasper spread my legs further apart to allow him full access, as he plunged into me with his fingers. Already, I was soaking wet with desire, achingly needing him inside me. Right then and there. Still, I was embarrassed to bring a voice to my needs as he continued tantalizing me, sliding in and out of me like a pendulum.

"Look at me, Angel," He said, when he came up for air. I could barely breathe, and still, I did as he commanded. "Yes, I want those eyes watching me, while I make you come."

Was he insane? I could barely keep my head up! I could feel my entire body begin to shiver in anticipation of his touch, as he stood up to grab a box of Trojan's out of his nightstand drawer.

For some reason, I found it convenient that he had them on hand and let myself wonder for a moment. *Had he expected this of me? Or perhaps they were there from someone else before?*

I quickly shoved that thought away, refusing to let any shred of doubt creep in and steal the glory of what was soon to come. Returning my focus to his desire burning just as hot as mine as he made quick work of applying the condom to his fully erect penis.

Staring deep into my eyes, he dared not blink as he entered inside me, sending a warm wave to flush over my skin as our bodies crashed together like a swell in the ocean. "Jasper..." I whimpered, as the lids of my eyes began to close in sweet ecstasy. Jasper swiftly silenced my cries with his lips and began kissing me with a passion unleashed from somewhere, deep within his soul. Crashing in and out of me, like the waves of a foreign shore, it felt as though the entire world was ours and ours alone.

As the rain pounded against his bedroom window, so did his body into me. I could live here forever, I thought to myself as I began to fantasize of some secret wormhole into another dimension that would keep us locked in this very moment for eternity.

Nothing would ever compare to how it felt, having him inside me, exploring every nook and cranny as he caught a rhythm of sweet perfection. The intensity slowly increased as my climax fostered its way towards reality.

Jasper brushed the unruly hair out of my eyes and kissed me so hard, as our bodies collided with one another. I swear my heart felt like it could beat right out of my chest. I nearly screamed out in pleasure!

It wasn't very long before I found my release. With half lidded eyes, I found Jasper watching my every move with an intensity that could make the earth shatter before me. He made sure I was good, before he, too, let himself go.

Falling to the side, we both lay there with our hearts rapidly beating in sync with one another. I lathered myself in the content state of being I was in. Surely, Jasper might be surprised if he knew that he had been the first to discover the experience of a true orgasm.

Even when the sex had been consensual, AJ was always far more concerned with getting himself off, leaving me hanging out to dry somewhere in the dust. I never knew that sex can be so pleasurable up until that very moment, and if I had my way, I was only just beginning to learn.

I fell fast asleep in Jasper's arms and like a rock, he never moved. Despite how safe and secure I felt in his embrace, my haunted subconscious mind had other plans.

The air was hot, so hot and thick. Sweating profusely, I couldn't sleep. I needed to get up for a glass of water. I opened my eyes, and pulled the comforter down off of my soaking, wet body. Dear God! What on earth was that smell? It was too dark for me to see anything, but I didn't want to wake him up. I swung my feet off, over the side of the bed and made my way over to the bathroom to find a towel to dry myself off with. I'd never sweat like this before.

I flicked on the light switch and turned on the faucet to splash some cold water on my face. When I turned my face to the mirror, I shrieked out in horror! It wasn't sweat I was dripping in, I was covered in blood! Frantically,

I began scrubbing my skin, but the blood was everywhere. I looked down, to find my nightgown was completely covered in it. I couldn't figure out why I was bleeding or where I was bleeding from. I turned off the light switch and went back to the bedroom to find my slippers, when I came across a scene that was easily straight out of a horror film.

He laid there, lifeless, pale as a ghost, covered in a pool of blood. Was it mine or his? I slowly pulled the covers down off of him and his body shot up so quickly, I was startled. "How could you do this to me?" AJ said, reaching out towards me with his hands. A butcher knife was pierced right through his heart. I screamed!

"Wake up, Carla." I could feel my body shifting back and forth. "You're having a nightmare." Jasper said, while quickly pulling me into his arms. "Are you alright?"

I gathered my thoughts for a moment, while catching my breath and I realized it was only a dream. "Yeah, I'm okay," I said, shakily, knowing damn well that I wasn't. "I'm sorry... I" Jasper silenced me by putting his finger on my lips.

"Please don't apologize, it was just a dream. Why don't I take you downstairs and get you something to drink." He said, shifting to his feet to get my clothes. He tossed them over to me to put on and slipped on a pair of boxer shorts.

"Yeah, okay." I replied, silently wondering if anyone had ever actually died of embarrassment before. I quickly got dressed and followed Jasper out of his master suite.

Chapter 40

A t some point in the night, Lucas must have made his way back upstairs because he was fast asleep, snoring in his bed when we passed by his crate. I followed Jasper down the spiral staircase and into the kitchen. He took two glasses down from the cabinet and poured us each a glass of cold milk.

"I guess now might be a good time for some chocolate cake, huh?" He said, attempting to lighten the mood. I certainly wasn't going to deny the opportunity to see if it was worth Jamie's hype.

"You won't ever see me turn down an opportunity for cake" I replied, catching his vibe. I glanced up at the time, displayed on the microwave. It was almost 2 am. *Shit! I forgot to text Jamie.* I walked over to the coffee table in the living room to find my cell phone where I'd left it earlier, while Jasper cut us each a hefty slice of cake.

Me

Fell asleep! Sorry, I forgot to text you, Don't wait up for me

Surely, she would already be sleeping. I didn't expect her to reply, but I did want her to find my text in the morning, so she wouldn't worry.

"This is fantastic! Did you bake this from scratch?" Jasper asked. I looked over to see him devour a huge bite of cake off of his fork. His satisfaction gave me all the feels, as I recalled how nervous I was to ensure the cake's perfection. "It's by far the best chocolate cake I've ever had." He said with his mouth full.

I quickly went back over to the kitchen and pulled out a stool to join him at the kitchen island counter. "Yes, I did, actually. I'm so glad you like it." I said, smiling as I watched him take a swig of milk from one of the glasses he poured us. The milk dribbled over his mustache and I couldn't help but giggle. I had to agree with Jasper as I scooped a forkful into my own mouth. A moist and fluffy piece of chocolate heaven, in each bite. Jasper brushed the back of his hand across his mouth to swipe away the milk, and I could swear, my stomach flip flopped. Even watching this man eat turned me on.

"So, my best friend, Jamie, made me promise to invite you over for a little party she's throwing for my birthday." After sharing everything I just did with this man, I don't know why I felt so shy to ask him about this. *Fear of rejection? Maybe.*

"Your birthday?" He asked.

"Well, it's actually on Tuesday, but she's inviting some of our friends over on Friday for game night and birthday cake." I said, hoping he didn't find it too lame.

"Why didn't you tell me? You know, I wouldn't miss it for the world,

Angel." He replied.

His answer swiftly tucked my nerves neatly into their drawers in my mind, where they belonged. After we finished our cake, Jasper and I went upstairs to try and get some sleep.

"So... Do you want to talk about it?" He asked, referring to my nightmare as we both lay awake in his bed.

My hesitation to his question ratted me out like a twelve year old. Jasper wasn't stupid, by any means. The 'don't insult my intelligence' expression he had spread across his face was clear in the pale moonlight dripping in from the window. That look busted the door wide open for me to allow myself to be vulnerable. I could no longer keep this looming secret between us. Any time I lied about it, I could feel the guilt gnawing its way into my psyche, more than I cared to allow. After the night we had just shared, I honestly felt closer to Jasper than ever. I only hoped I wasn't being too naive, to believe that I could trust him enough to open up about how things truly went down, between AJ and me. After all, I had just shared my full naked body with his, how could this be much different? *It's your emotions, Carla, not your body.*

"I'm not so sure where to start." I said, swallowing the lump in my throat. I took a deep breath in and gave it my best. "First, you have to promise me, that what I am about to tell you, you won't freak out."

When Jasper agreed not to overreact, I proceeded to tell him about my relationship with AJ and how I wound up coming to Boston. I spared him a good amount of the fine details because I didn't want to stir him up to the point of breaking his agreement with me. By the time I finished, I had let him know enough to fully understand that I'd

216

just gotten out of a relationship with an alcoholic, narcissist who had mentally, physically and sexually abused me.

After allowing Jasper a few minutes to digest, I gave him a vivid description of the nightmare I had while it was still fresh on my mind. I was surprised at how much better I felt, once I let it all out on the line for him.

Knowing I wasn't the one to blame for everything didn't change how ashamed I felt of it all. I didn't want to sound like a victim, because in my eyes, I was courageous enough to fight back, by leaving AJ when I did.

Jasper sharply inhaled through his nose, as his jaw clenched in anger, right before he reached over and pulled me into his arms. Despite the fiery rage, igniting in Jasper's beautiful eyes, he did his best to keep his promise. "You're safe now. That's all that matters. And I promise you this, if that asshole ever comes near you again, he will regret the day he was ever born."

Somehow, the words he spoke held the power to make me feel safe, while also chilling me to the bone. Deep down, I had no doubt that he meant every syllable to every word he spoke. Still I felt as vulnerable as a perfectly ripened peach, dangling low on the branch of a tree, waiting for someone to yank me off and feast on me. A place I was completely unfamiliar, nor comfortable with.

Detecting my discomfort, Jasper traveled the galaxy far and wide to rescue me from the endangered planet I had somehow landed on and opened up to me about his birth mom. He laced his hands through mine, intertwining our fingers as he poured out his own heart to me.

"After my father passed, my mom began using drugs to cope with her grief. Inevitably, she, began dating her drug dealer who only used her for her money. I was only five then, but I knew he wasn't any good for her. If she didn't give him what he wanted, he would often get violent with her. One day, he took me away from her for several days."

All ears, I watched his eyes veer off to the left as he continued. "I remember staying at some cheap motel. There were several women who had come and gone in the time that we were there." Jasper paused as he tried to recollect the details he had seemingly locked away for quite some time.

"I mostly sat on the other bed watching cartoons while he and these other women got high and had sex." Jasper chuckled before continuing. "I guess I should probably be thankful that he fed me and was gracious enough to tell me to turn the other way." The image he painted in my mind had instantly brought tears to my eyes. I let them fall silently, as I tried not to make a sound, so he could continue without interruption.

"When we finally went back home, my mother was in rough shape. She looked as though she had been crying for days. It was only a few weeks later, that my mother died of an overdose."

Trying to imagine what that must have been like for Jasper was hard, but it did ring similarly with my own early childhood with my mom and my birth dad.

"That must have been awful, I can't imagine how that must have been for you as a little boy," I said, consolingly. I removed my hand from his and softly tousled his hair.

"My father never cheated on my mother, but I can remember waiting in the car for him for what seemed like hours while he went inside bars to drink." I confessed as I came to the realization that it may have been at this time where I had developed this relationship with my father, inside my head. I could recall myself as a young girl, begging him to return to the car in my mind as I waited. That relationship carried on through the years, long after my mother took me away from him.

"I think there may be some sort of psychological connection to the sudden loss of my physical relationship with my father to the reason why I stayed with AJ as long as I had. I must have believed, subconsciously, that If I could manage to save AJ, I might also be able to save my dad."

"Trying to save someone is no reason to stay and let them continue to abuse you, but I can understand why you might have felt that way." Jasper said, while brushing his thumb along my temple. "The truth is, the only person who can truly save us, is ourselves." He said wisely, while pulling me in closer to hold me tight. I hated to admit it, but Jasper was right.

My father lost his mother to illness when he was nine. As I got older, I naturally attributed my father's alcoholism to his own childhood trauma, letting him off the hook for any damage he'd caused me. Beyond the neglect I suffered while he was drunk, he was still my world.

His disability kept him home with me more than my mom. I knew he loved me. I felt it in the things he did for me, like teaching me how to make my bed and sweep the floor. I felt his love when he would tuck me into bed each night, while my mother worked three jobs to support us. It believed it was the demon of his alcoholism that led him to neglect my needs to secure his own. I held my father high on a pedestal, because beyond the surface, I felt a love that was genuine. What I didn't know was that by letting my own father off the hook, I had also left the door wide open, to allow the abuse I had suffered with AJ.

It wasn't like me to be so open about my deepest emotions, yet Jasper somehow drew it out of me, like magic. This was far from the average topic of discussion, for a first date. The similarity of our past was far from being lost on me. It led me to wonder if our meeting was somehow supernatural. *Were we predestined to meet? Maybe Jasper would help me heal my scars from AJ?* My mind was flooded with all these thoughts as I drifted off to sleep in the comfort of his arms.

Chapter 41

The sunlight blanketed the room like it was high up in the sky, as I awoke in Jasper's bed. I reached my hand across his side of the bed to find that it was warm, but also empty. I pulled the blanket down and sat myself up, pulling my knees inward to my chest as I took a second to glance around the room. *Maybe he's in the shower?*

After letting my feet fall to the soft woolen carpeted floor, I noticed a white card stock paper with my name written on it that had been folded in half so that it would stand up on the nightstand, by my side of the bed. *Aww, Jasper left me a note.* I took a moment to embrace the feeling of warmth that flowed inside me. I was extremely curious to see what he had written, and wasted no time at all in reading it.

Hi Angel,

You were sleeping so peacefully, I couldn't bring myself to wake you. Last night was beautiful, even better than I could have ever imagined. Lucas and I picked up some fresh croissants for breakfast when we went for our walk this morning. You'll find them on the breakfast bar. Please make yourself at home and feel free to stay as long as you like. I will be back later this afternoon. Text me when you wake up!

Jasper

How sweet of him to write me a note. *Angel was a term* of endearment I could certainly get used to. Like a shot of dopamine, it sent tingles right through me. You know, the kind that made me feel like I was special to him. In most cases, I would have felt ashamed to have given myself so freely to a guy on the first date, both physically and emotionally, but with Jasper it was very different. The note he left me gave me more than enough confidence to banish any doubt my mind might let wander into.

~

When I walked out of Jasper's bedroom, I was already showered and dressed. I found Lucas lying on the love-seat upstairs in the loft. Both of his ears perked up when he heard me open the door.

"Hey buddy." I said as the little nub of his tail got to wagging. I sat down on the love-seat to pet Lucas for a minute until it dawned on me that I had completely missed my self defense class with Jamie this morning. *Shit! Jamie's gonna kill me!*

I quickly ran down the spiral staircase and down into the kitchen. Lucas, sensing my excitement, followed right behind me. There was a box of assorted croissants on the kitchen Island, just as Jasper

222

mentioned in the note. Next to the box of croissants was my cell phone, where I'd left it the night before. By now, Jamie would surely be worried, so I quickly picked it up to call her and let her know I was alright.

My battery was low, but I could still see that I had eight missed calls. Two from Jamie this morning, five from my mother and one more from my sister, Abby. An eerie feeling crept over me, it wasn't like my mother to call me so many times. Normally she'd give me a few hours and call back. I didn't have a chance to read the text messages I had missed before my phone began to ring again. This time it was Abby calling me again. Something was wrong, I could feel it. Whatever reason my mother may have been calling me for, Abby was sure to know about it, so I hit the accept button on the call.

"There you are, baby…." The voice on the other line sent chills down my spine, and not in a good way. I knew that voice from anywhere, and it certainly wasn't my sister, Abby's. That voice belonged to the evil demon dwelling inside AJ Stratton. Stunned quiet, my voice had completely left my throat. It felt like a rat was gnawing away at my guts as the air began to slowly escape my lungs.

"What's the matter, cat got your tongue, eh? You didn't think I would miss your birthday, did you?" He said, laughing as though he were delighting in my present misery. *What the hell was he doing with Abby's phone?*

My heart began racing as I managed to wrangle up enough air to take a breath. "How did you get this number?" I asked to the tune of even more laughter on the other end of the line.

"Wait a minute, wait a minute-" more laughter on the line "there's someone else here who wants to wish you a happy birthday, too" He said. I could hear him breathing into the phone as if he were pacing around. A minute later, I heard, "Carla, he's got a gun! Please don't let him kill me!" It was Abby's voice, clear as day! Then I could hear her muffled shouting as if he were holding his hand over her mouth or worse, taping it shut.

"That's enough!" AJ shouted. "It's a shame, you know. We're getting ready for your birthday surprise and you're not even home to see it."

"Don't you touch her! Don't you touch her!" I yelled, tears stinging in my eyes, and a burning sensation at the back of my throat. "It's me you want, let her go, please AJ!" I said, pleading for Abby's life. *I could kill him myself!*

"You'd better get here quick then... Oh, and Carla, don't you even think about calling anyone else, or your sweet little sister, Abby will die!" He said. quickly hitting the end button on the call.

As soon as the line went dead, I immediately redialed Abby's number, but there was no answer on the call. I quickly grabbed my purse and made a dash for the elevator. My mind was racing like an athlete who had been training for a triathlon. A million thoughts crashed over me as I envisioned Abby tied up somewhere in my old apartment with AJ hanging over her at gunpoint. *Dear God, please don't let him touch her the way he did me.* I ran straight past Charlie, the security guard, and into the parking garage.

"Are you alright, Miss Carla?" I heard him calling out after me, but it didn't even register in my mind to respond. All I could think about was Abby and the terrible danger she was in at the hands of AJ. I got in my car and hit the highway.

The only piece of comfort I had in me was the fact that I knew it was me that he wanted, *not Abby.* I clung to that thought fort for dear life as I raced my way back to Virginia. I knew I had to get there quickly, the less time he had with her, the less damage there would be. *He wouldn't really hurt her would he?* The truth was, I honestly didn't know just how far AJ would go. Heaven forbid he was drunk or high, God only knew! I prayed the whole way... *Please don't hurt Abby!*

Chapter 42

Jasper

The little coo coo bird made his call, as the clock struck one, when I came home from the office. The clock belonged to my grandfather, one of the very few possessions I had left from my parents. It was also the very first adornment to the wall when I first moved into my apartment. Lucas greeted me at the elevator. "Hey Boy" I said, giving him a quick pat on the head.

A quick glance around suggested that Carla might still be upstairs sleeping. She never sent me a text this morning and her sweater was still sprawled out, across the couch. The croissants were still left out on the island counter, untouched from this morning, where I'd left them for her.

Although it seemed pretty late for her to still be sleeping, I gave her the benefit of the doubt. After all, we were up half the night. I figured I could bring her breakfast upstairs in bed, so I brewed some coffee. I hadn't the slightest clue as to how she took her coffee. I decided to pour it black and set it on a tray with some cream and sugar, along with a few croissants on a plate and a small glass of orange juice.

I was surprised when I made it up the stairs that Carla was nowhere to be found. I quickly glanced at the nightstand. Evidently, she saw the note I left her because it, too, was gone. Something in the pit of my stomach told me that something was wrong. For the sake of not driving myself insane, I had to let it go, telling myself I would see her later.

I wanted to give her the space she might be needing, so I decided not to call her just yet. It was the waiting that was hard. All I really needed was to know that she was alright, at the very least. I didn't want to push things too far with her. *Damn it! I knew I should have waited until she was ready.* She was so nervous, though. Naturally, all I wanted to do was try and help her relax.

I finally settled on an idea to head back to Silver Linings to see if she made it to work. If I could just see her face, I would know that she was okay. Since no one in the office had been aware of us dating, and we had yet to discuss that part of our relationship, I would just have to make it seem like I was there for something else.

My heart sank when I found Aunt Maggie at the front desk answering the phones. *She should be here by now. Damn! Maybe she's just late?*

"I thought you left already." Maggie said, looking surprised to see me.

"I did, I had to come back to finish something I was working on." I didn't know what to tell her. Attempting to buy some time to stick around, I gave her my vague response, hoping she was busy enough to not look any further into it.

"You know, I've always admired your dedication, but sometimes you work too hard! I'm sure that whatever it is, it could've waited until tomorrow." She laughed.

A call came through, breaking Maggie's attention away from me. *Thank God!* I took the opportunity and ran with it. Dodging Maggie's inquisition, I briskly walked back to my office where I closed the door behind me.

I could wait in here for a little while, just to see if she shows up for her shift. It wasn't like me to think so irrationally, but I was honestly worried. I don't know why I was worried, I could just feel it rotting away in my stomach, like I'd eaten some spoiled food.

It wasn't like there hadn't been any other women in my life. The fact was, there were far too many to count. It wasn't anything I was proud of. Each of them were nameless faces with no significance, other than a means to an end, to satisfy my urges. And still, not a single one of them had ever awakened me the way Carla did. I felt drawn to her like no one else before. The mere thought of her brought me to life... Like I had been sleeping the whole time, right up until I saw that tear stained, angel face of hers run past me, the night of the premier of the club. I knew that she was fragile. All I wanted, was to be near her and to keep her safe.

When Lucas found her at the park, I just knew we were destined to meet. When I found out she had been living in the same building as me, it only solidified the fact that it was fate. I knew she was clearly distraught, the way she ran for her life at the mere mention of the bruise on her face. That's why I kept my distance. It was why I waited so long to reveal my identity to her... It killed me, but I just knew she wasn't ready.

The worst thing you could do while waiting for time to pass is watch the damn clock. I knew this, and yet I still caught myself checking my watch, every five minutes. The window of my office gave a full view of the driveway and I had yet to see Carla's car pull in. *Where could she be?*

When five o'clock rolled around, I submitted to the fact that she probably wasn't coming in to work and decided to head home. I figured by now, enough time had passed and it wouldn't hurt to send her a quick text message.

Me

Hey you. Where did you go?

Radio silence was all I got back. *Had I pushed her too far? Man, I really hope I didn't blow my chance!*

~

When I got home, I saw Charlie sitting at the front desk. "Hey Charlie." I said, as I walked through the door of the lobby. For a minute, I thought about asking him if he'd seen her, but I didn't want to seem like some crazy stalker. It was bad enough, I had asked him to hand her all those gifts, with no card attached. God only knew what he thought of me already.

"Jasper? Is that you?" Jamie awkwardly asked me, as she emerged from the elevator. She tucked her long, brown hair behind her ear when she halted at the security desk, where Charlie and I were talking.

"Yes... I'm guessing you're Jamie?" I asked, hoping I was right.

"Yes, I'm Jamie. I'm Carla's roommate. Well, she's my best friend... I'm looking for Carla. She never came home. I got a text from her last night when she was with you, but I haven't seen or heard from her since. Her mother called me this morning to tell me her little sister, Abby, went missing." Jamie spewed out in a fit of panic. "I'm afraid she may be in great danger!"

"Excuse me, I don't mean to pry, but is Miss Carla in some sort of trouble?" Charlie asked, quickly chiming in. His voice was drenched in concern. "She left out of here in a hurry, this morning. I thought something may have been wrong the way she ran out of here, without saying hello."

"Christ! Was she driving, Charlie? What time did she leave?" I asked.

"She sped out of here so fast, she left tracks out in the garage. I wasn't here for very long, so it had to be around 11 AM." He replied.

"Do me a favor, find the security footage of her leaving. I need her license plate number. Can you do that for me, Charlie?" I asked, pulling my phone out of my pocket to make a call. I quickly found Tony's name in my contacts and pressed the send button for the call.

"Of course," Charlie quickly agreed.

"Has she told you anything about AJ?" Jamie asked, wondering how lightly she should tread on Carla's privacy, at this point.

"Yes, she did. I don't know about you, but I'm not waiting around to find out if he's involved in this." I answered, in a clipped tone.

"Hi, Tony. It's Jasper. Did Carla ever show up for work today?" I figured I would ask, hoping it was all some weird misunderstanding. Tony and I were friends. I confided in him about my interest with Carla on Friday, after her welcome party. He was the only one in the office who knew. He told me to go for it, because he'd never seen me this excited about a girl before.

"No, she hasn't been here since Friday." Tony replied. "I was wondering why she-"

"I need you to do me a big favor, please." I said, cutting in, "I have reason to believe she might be in trouble. Can you find her last known address for me please?"

"You know that's classified information, I could get fired." he said.

"Please, Tony... it's an emergency! I think her life may be in danger." I pleaded.

"Okay, okay, I'll see what I can find. I'll call you back when I find it."

"Thanks Tony," I ended the call, returning my attention to Jamie.

"Jamie, I need to know everything you do know about AJ. Do you think there's any chance he might be behind all of this?"

"I only met him a few times. He seemed pretty normal to me, when I met him a couple of years ago, but after seeing what he did to her and all the nightmares she's been having, I have no doubt, this has *everything* to do with him." Jamie responded, clearly shaken up. "I'll see if I can get her address from her mother. Are you planning on going down there to look for her?" Jamie asked.

"She had a nightmare last night when she was with me..." I murmured, more to myself than to Carla's friend, Jamie. My blood began to boil with anger. "I don't know how I'm going to do it, but I will find her!"

To be continued...

Find out what happens next, in book 2 of the Silver Linings Trilogy.
Silver Linings:
SECRETS
By: Elisa Ann Pratt

About the Author

Originally born in Queens, NY, Elisa Ann Pratt currently resides in south Florida with her husband, two teenage sons and three fur babies. She deals cards for a living full time, while pursuing her passion for writing.

Her talent was first noticed by friends and family when she began writing poetry as a little girl. In middle school, one of her poems won a contest, landing a spot in the school newspaper.

In high school, she took several creative writing courses and wrote poetry and short stories for fun, mostly entertaining her friends, but also utilized her writing as an outlet for her most inner thoughts. She always knew she was a writer, life just seemed to get in the way, as it does for many.

Elisa has always been a hard worker, taking pride in the various hats she wore as a young adult where she sometimes worked three jobs to make ends meet.

On social media, you'll find she loves to cook, listen to music, take photos and read books. She truly believes we are all gifted with our own unique talent to share with the world and goes out of her way to support anyone with courage to chase their own dreams and aspirations.

Elisa finally feels she is in the right place to showcase her writing to a greater audience where she hopes to relate to, entertain and inspire others.

Stay tuned for Book 2 in the Silver Linings Series
   Follow me for updates at: Linktr.ee/elisaannpratt

Social media links

Also by Elisa Ann Pratt

Being a published author is my dream come true. I want to express my deepest gratitude to my readers for being the greatest part of my journey. Without you, none of this is possible.

If you or someone you know is struggling with domestic abuse, please know there are resources available that can help you.

National Domestic Abuse Hot Line

Available 24/7

English and Spanish and 200+ other languages with interpretation services

phone: 800-799-7233

SMS: Text START to 88788

www.ingramcontent.com/pod-product-compliance
Lightning Source LLC
Chambersburg PA
CBHW022039240626

47154CB00007B/2477